Sundown Comes Twice

Judd Miller and his brother work to start a small ranch outside the town of Red Bluffs. But other interests in their valuable property lead to the powerful mayor of the town, working with other crooked officials, to fleece the brothers of their deeded ground, culminating in the killing of Judd's brother, Randall. Unknown to Judd, the transcontinental railroad is coming through, with an interest in buying his property to shorten their route through the mountains.

Judd flees attempts to kill him, turning instead to a gunfighter to avenge Randall's death, while exposing the men who conspired against him. Can a young widow and a reformed preacher be enough to battle and beat the odds?

Sundown Comes Twice

Art Isberg

A Black Horse Western

ROBERT HALE

© Art Isberg 2019
First published in Great Britain 2019

ISBN 978-0-7198-3021-1

The Crowood Press
The Stable Block
Crowood Lane
Ramsbury
Marlborough
Wiltshire SN8 2HR

www.bhwesterns.com

Robert Hale is an imprint
of The Crowood Press

The right of Art Isberg to be identified as
author of this work has been asserted by him
in accordance with the Copyright, Designs and
Patents Act 1988

Typeset by
Derek Doyle & Associates, Shaw Heath
Printed and bound in Great Britain by
4Bind Ltd, Stevenage, SG1 2XT

CHAPTER ONE

The blazing white, sun-bleached desert was interrupted only by tall-armed saguaro cactus reaching for the sky as if praying for rain that would never come. A sidewinder rattlesnake quickly S-curved across burning sands to the safety of shade under a rocky outcrop. Nothing else seemed alive or moved except the slow advance of shadows cast by the blistering midday sun. But something else was moving, coming slowly closer: the filmy figure of a horse and rider making its way through shimmering waves of heat. The man wore a sweat-soaked, wide-brimmed hat pulled low across his face, his eyes mere slits against the blinding glare. Judd Miller was still alive, still in the saddle trying to outrun and outride the five-man posse that had dogged his trail for nearly a week. Were they still back there, he wondered, or had they finally given up and turned back to the safety and shady heights of hill country where the chase had started?

Judd eased back on the reins, pulling the big bay

horse to a stop. Getting down he stood in the thin shadow of a tall saguaro, wiping his sweat-soaked face with the back of his shirt sleeve. Squinting back the way he'd come, Miller stood for a long time studying his back trail. Lean and bone-dry thirsty, Judd Miller had one unusual thing about his appearance: although right-handed, he wore his six-gun on his left hip, pistol butt forward, favouring a cross-draw.

Nothing stirred. It seemed that at long last the hanging posse had finally given up and turned back. He took in a deep breath of relief. Lifting one of two canvas water bags looped over the saddle horn, he shook its liquid contents. The quiet splash said nearly empty. One long gulp finished it. Pulling the plug off the second, he took off his hat, half filling it, holding it for his horse to drink from.

'That's it for a while,' he patted the tall animal on the neck.

'No telling when we'll find more to fill up these bags. Let's rest for a while before we move again. We've both earned it.'

Many miles back Jared Bass pulled to a halt, peering out intently across the desert in front of him. He cursed bitterly under his breath, trying to think of something to say to the four men riding with him. One of them spoke up before he could.

'Looks like he's gone, someplace out there, Jared,' the man shook his head. 'The desert will finish him off even if we couldn't, that's for sure.'

'Yeah,' another chimed in. 'Let's get out of this

God forsaken country and turn for home. Even a horny toad would fry in this heat. No man can stick it.'

A third rider pushed his hat back on his head, eyeing his pals. 'Besides that, the thousand dollar reward split five ways means we'd only get two hundred each. The longer we have to ride chasing him, the smaller that money gets. If we keep at this, it's hardly worth it any more. Let the buzzards and coyotes finish him. He'll never see another sundown, that's for sure.'

Bass still stared across the savage landscape, the grim look of failure playing across his stubbled face. He was tempted to tell the rest of them to turn back, and keep riding on his own. Miller was only flesh and bone, just like any other man. If he was still riding out there, so could he. It galled him to admit defeat, and to have to give up and return home to Red Bluffs empty handed. For him, the money was only part of the reason why he wanted Judd Miller dead without any thought of a judge, jury or trial. Too much might come out at a trial that could implicate the man he worked for, Mayor Cyrus Toomey.

Toomey didn't want a trial either. That's why he'd sent this posse out in the first place, to finish off Judd and leave his body to rot without it ever being found. The Miller name had haunted the mayor for more reasons than one. Judd's brother Randall had been ambushed one night riding home from town, and killed by unknown assailants. Randall had been in a hurry to tell his brother some stunning news that

7

he'd just learned regarding the ranch property they'd recently purchased and were building into a place of their own. His murder meant that secret died with him.

On a more personal note, Toomey's daughter, Rachel, had become romantically involved with Randall over the previous few months, and her father could not stop it, try as he might. Toomey had big plans for himself to move up in the political world, the mayorship of Red Bluffs being just the first step along the way. He wasn't about to jeopardize his climb by allowing his daughter to get more involved with a struggling small-time rancher like Randall and his brother Judd, trying to make a go of their property. How would it look when whispers of breeding and background began tittering through social settings and smoky back rooms, where deals were cut and political decisions made. It all came to a head one evening, just days before Randall was killed.

'I'm ordering you to stop seeing this cowboy, and I mean right now, today. Do you hear me, Rachel? I'm demanding it, by God!' he shouted, red-faced, the blood vessels distended on his fat neck.

Rachel held her ground. She had known this confrontation was coming, and wasn't about to let her father bully her into submission. 'Do you think I'm a child you can order around, like you did my mother? I will not let you do that to me. I'm twenty years old and I know what I want in my life. Don't try and tell me who I can and cannot see – not now or at any other time!'

'I'll cut you off without a dime if you don't listen to me. So help me, I will!'

'You do, and I'll pack up and move in with Randall and his brother. How would you like that attached to your untarnished name? Your daughter living in sin with two brothers just outside town. I'll do it, I swear I will!'

Cyrus's hand came up as if to strike a blow. He caught himself shaking with rage, and instead picked up a picture of his deceased wife, hurling it across the room, the glass frame shattering in the fireplace. One last glare at Rachel, and he stormed out of the room.

The sudden, unexplained murder of 'Randy' Miller, as everyone called him, had sent shock waves through the citizens in Red Bluffs. He was a likeable, outgoing young man, with the drive to make something of the new piece of ground he and his brother had purchased. But like all brothers, they argued from time to time, and unfortunately had done so just days before his death, while in town buying supplies. A number of people present had heard the disagreement, part of it over Rachel. When Cyrus Toomey heard about it he acted quickly, ordering the arrest of Judd on suspicion of murder, even though he knew better.

Jared Bass had made the mistake of riding out to the Miller ranch to take him in, with only a phony badge and a young deputy, Evan Dixon, backing him up. When Jared confronted Miller at his door, Judd had accused him of being a stooge of Toomey's, and to get off his property. Bass had tried to force the issue until Judd had grabbed the shotgun he kept next to the front door, levelling it on Bass.

'You come back out here and try this again, I'll give you the wrong end of this shotgun. Now get off my property. You can tell your boss what I said, too.'

Bass had backed up with both hands in the air, staring with alarm at the gaping barrels on the shotgun, along with wide-eyed Dixon. 'I'll be back. Next time with enough guns to put a rope around your neck!'

'You do, and you'll wish you never tried,' Judd had warned one last time. 'Even you can't be crazy enough to think I'd kill my own brother. Get going!'

But Judd knew that Bass would try again. That night he sat in the darkened cabin by the window, looking out into the night. Randall had been murdered for some unknown reason, and now Red Bluffs law wanted to take him, Judd Miller, in for it. None of it made any sense, yet somehow he knew they had to be connected. The only thing he was certain of was that he wasn't going to allow anyone to try hangman's law.

The hours passed slowly and the night grew still, except for the lonesome call of a coyote somewhere out in the dark. The only other sound was the steady tick-tick-ticking of the clock on the fireplace mantel, which he couldn't see. Judd took in a deep breath, closing his eyes for a moment to rest, fighting back the overwhelming urge to sleep. Maybe he was wrong about Bass showing up at night. It was already late.

Maybe he'd try it tomorrow. Maybe. . . .

He suddenly sat straight up, opening his eyes again, searching for the strange sound he'd just heard. Now he heard it again, the sound of hard-soled boots slipping slowly closer over gravelly ground. He leaned closer to the window until dark shadows materialized out of the night, the outline of two men advancing at a crouch on the front door.

'Get back!' Judd shouted, jumping to his feet, thrusting the shotgun out of the window. Both men suddenly fired six-guns, the brilliant gun flashes lighting the night and briefly themselves. Judd fired a ball of flame lasting just long enough to see one man throw up his hands, then fall to the ground with a pitiful moan. The second turned to run. Judd fired the second barrel, cutting him down in mid-stride, before all hell broke loose. Pistol and rifle fire erupted from a line of men hidden just yards away in front of the cabin, forcing Judd to dive to the floor, bullets thudding into the front wall, holing the door and shattering the other front window. A coal oil lamp on a shelf shattered, spilling the liquid down the wall.

Miller was half way across the room when a flaming torch spiralled through the night, landing with a thud against the outside wall. A second quickly followed, then a third, until flames licked up the wall and through the window, igniting the coal oil inside with a rush of hot air. Shouts outside demanded he give up, as he reached the back door. Getting to his feet with the empty shotgun still in his hands, he

11

reached for the door handle. Throwing it open he saw two more men running around the side of the house to block him from escaping.

Judd didn't hesitate: his cross draw pulled up the .45, firing once, twice, and a third time, both men going down before they could fire back. The pole corral stood a short sprint away. He dashed for it, mounting his horse that he had saddled earlier that evening in case something unexpected like this happened. He kicked the tall horse away with one last look back at the cabin now roaring with flames, as more wild shots rang out after him.

That fateful night put Judd Miller's name and face on wanted posters as a killer, on the run with a reward on his head. For the first time in his life he found himself on the wrong side of the law, being hunted like a wild animal, forced to flee into the desolation of the desert, not knowing where he was. He knew he could not go back to Red Bluffs as only a hangman's rope waited for him there. Judd decided his best bet was to keep riding farther out into this bitter land until he found water or some sign of civilization.

The posse arrived back in town six days later, to the relief of all riders except Jared Bass. He had to face Toomey, and he wasn't looking forward to it, for good reason. The mayor quickly began berating him the minute he stepped into his office.

'You mean you let him get away . . . all five of you!' Cyrus stormed around the room shaking his head, throwing dagger glances at Bass, who stood in front of the desk avoiding eye contact, as the Canyon City stagecoach rattled by outside.

'Listen, Cyrus, we ended up a week south of here down in desert country. You don't know what that's like. It's nothing but heat and rattlesnakes. No man can track anyone over that stony ground. Besides, it's likely Miller is dead by now. We damn near died ourselves trying to run him down.'

'He better be, or someone might end up being hung, you want to guess who? I'm going to get that property of his under foreclosure, or any other way I can. That's what started this whole mess in the first place. I could have hung him by now and be done with all this until you let him get away.'

That evening Rachel Toomey sat on the bed in her room, her face buried in a handkerchief, sobbing quietly over Randall's brutal murder. The emotional collapse that she had endured since his death was only worsened by the fear that her father might have had a hand in it. He had threatened her about seeing the young man – could he actually have carried out that threat with a death sentence? The question haunted her. Slowly the tears stopped and she dried her eyes, knowing that she had to find out – otherwise, not knowing the answer, she knew she would go insane.

Cyrus was sitting at his desk in the small office in his home when she walked in; at the click of the door handle he looked up from the paperwork he was reading, and one look at Rachel's face was all it took

13

for him to prepare himself for what he knew was coming.

'You look terrible, Rachel. Why don't you have a cup of hot tea, and try to get some sleep?' He tried to cut her off before another argument started.

'I haven't been able to sleep since Randall was murdered.' She approached the desk, leaning with both hands on its surface, staring at her father without blinking. 'I want to ask you something, and I want a straight answer.'

Toomey locked eyes with her, knowing the question even before she asked it.

'All right, Rachel, I'll answer whatever you want if it will help calm you down. What is it, dear?'

'I want to know . . if you had anything to do with Randall's death – anything, even in the remotest way. Tell me the truth. I have to hear it for my own sanity.'

Toomey got up. Coming around the desk, he put both hands on Rachel's shoulders, pulling her so close he could feel her breath on his face.

'Of course I didn't. Do you think your father is some kind of a monster because we had a little disagreement?' He wrapped both arms around her, pulling her even closer – but with a small smile on his face that she never saw.

Judd's second water bag was down to the last dregs of the precious liquid when he reined to a stop, studying what looked like a thin veil of dust rising still some distance away but coming in his general direction. Was it just another spinning dust devil? He

urged the big bay forwards to get closer and inter-
cept its line of travel. In less than a mile he came to
a rough wagon track, the first sign of anything man-
made since his run from Red Bluffs, a week earlier.
Now he could make out that the growing black dot
was some sort of wagon. In a few minutes more he
saw it was a wagon pulled by a mule, the figure of a
man at the reins wearing a tall, black top hat. When
the wagon rattled to a stop, Judd got his first close-up
look at the driver, who was surely strange in appearance. He was an older man, tall and thin, wearing a
dusty black suit and, as Judd had already made out, a
well worn, silk hat. His weathered, unshaven face had
a thick growth of black stubble, which had all but
overgrown the remnants of a thin moustache.

'Howdy, neighbour!' The wagon man lifted his hat
with a smile. 'Fancy meeting another one of God's
children way out here. The Israelites may have spent
forty years wandering in the desert, but they didn't
do it here, or they'd still be at it!' He laughed at his
own joke. 'What would be your name, brother, if you
don't mind me asking you?'

'I'm called Judd Miller.'

'Well, Judd Miller, I propose we find some nice
shady spot and retire from this devil's furnace until
sundown gives us mere mortals a little rest. I haven't
seen another white man out here in a long time. We
can jaw for a while. What do you say to that?'

'If you know a place like that, I'd say it's a good
idea. And what is your name?'

'Mine? Well, I've given up the name my sweet

15

mother gave me, and decided to take one from the Lord. I call myself Moses Canaan, and have done so for a lot of years.'

'So you're a man of the Good Book?'

'I am. I only came to it as an adult, to change my wicked ways whoring around after fallen doves, drinking the Devil's brew of rye whiskey, and cheating at parlour games. I was real mean, once upon a time. I had a bible in one hand and a bottle in the other. I had to do something or die young. But I'm saved now, good as gold. This desert around us has become my Promised Land. I minister to anyone and all who need it. You see the sign on my wagon, don't you? It means what is says: 'Repent, or Hell Fire Will Be Your Reward!'

'I haven't seen another living soul since I've been out here except you, today. Who do you minister to?'

'There are scattered Indians that live out here, and sometimes I go into Dry Wells and give a Sunday service.'

'You mean there's a town someplace around here?'

'Yes, but not much of a one. Just a few stores for local folks. Last year I even performed a wedding!'

'How far away is it?'

'See those mountains over there?' He pointed to the rocky range. 'Dry Wells is right at the foot of them, about two days' ride from here. If you're still around for a few days, I'll take you in with me, so you can see it for yourself.'

16

'That I'd like to do. Do you live out here some-place?'

'I do. Tie your horse to my wagon, and join me up here on the front seat. I'll show you my place.'

The big-wheeled church wagon headed for a rocky canyon several miles away, while Judd sat on the spring seat eyeing his strange new acquaintance, wondering what other surprises he might come up with. He wasn't disappointed when the wagon creaked into a steep-walled canyon, coming to a stop in front of a large cave.

'Here it is, my home.' Moses swung his arm toward the entrance, with a smile on his face. 'I believe the Good Lord put it here for me to find and prosper in. I have a little pole corral around the bend we can put your horse and my mule in. When they're put up we can get inside out of this heat and relax. I'm about parched dry and need a good, cool drink of water to wet my whistle. How about you?'

'Yes, I am. My last water bag is just about empty. Do you have enough for me to fill both my bags?'

'Your two and a thousand more just like them, thanks to the providence of the Lord. Once we get inside I'll show you why.'

CHAPTER TWO

The big cave went well back in solid rock, and the temperature dropped dramatically into being almost cold. Judd marvelled at the sudden change. Near the end he could hear the steady *drip-drip* of water. Approaching the sound he found a fissure in the wall where repeated drops of water fell into a rocky bowl hollowed out by the endless passage of time. Next to it stood a large metal container filled to the top with cold, sweet water. A tin cup hung on one handle. Judd couldn't help but lick his lips at the sight of it. Moses saw his reaction.

'Go ahead, drink as much of it as you want. Soon as you're done, it will fill right back up again. By the way, if you don't mind me saying so, the way you keep that pistol on your hip is one I've never seen before. I saw right off you're right-handed, but you wear it on your left with the pistol butt forward.'

'I use a cross draw. Not many men do, but I find it's better for me, and faster too.'

'Sure looks mighty odd, but I'm no man of the

gun. I use my bible to bring men around to my way of thinking.

'Your way is probably better. Now let me get that drink. I've been dreaming about one for quite a while.'

The cave had a large stone-stocked fire pit near the entrance, a wooden bed roughly made out of tree limbs criss-crossed with leather thongs and topped by several blankets for comfort. A large, flat rock served as a table next to a pair of wooden chairs made in the same style as the bed frame. On the opposite wall, canned goods and glass jars sat on a rocky shelf serving as an open pantry. As Judd took it all in, he realized Moses had made quite a place for himself in this land of desolation and smoking hot heat.

'Well, what do you think of all this, Judd Miller?' Moses smiled.

'I'd say you've done pretty well for yourself. I'm surprised anything like this even exists.'

'Oh, I didn't do this. The Good Lord showed me the way to it. I was just like you, wandering around praying I'd find a drop of water to drink. I only made the few things you see here after I moved in. Now how about you? What are you doing out here in what some men call no man's land? We both know this is a place only a few men ever come to, and most of them do so not to be found, if you know what I mean. Does that idea fit you, too?'

Judd didn't answer right away, even though he didn't believe that his strange new friend posed a risk of any kind. After a long, odd silence, he locked eyes on Moses.

'Let's just say I'm out here because I have to be, at least for now. My reason for it is too long, with too many twists to try and explain.'

Moses let the words sink in a moment before trying one more question.

'Do you mind me asking if you have a family some-place, back wherever you came from?'

'I had a brother. He was ambushed and killed. That's as much as I want to say about it.'

'I understand. I won't intrude any further. I had a brother once too, before I lost him in the war. He fought for the rebs, and a gallant young man he was, before a Yankee bullet shattered his heart. That's when I left home and came out west, here. I didn't want any part of what was going on. It cost me my brother to realize that, and to change my wild ways, too. It was a pretty steep price to pay, and I'm still paying for it.'

That evening the two men sat watching the dancing flames rise higher in the fire pit, as the night-time temperatures began to drop, and Moses rambled on about his desert home.

'Funny, isn't it. The sun is so hot in day time it can drive you blind, then after sundown the desert turns so cold you'd almost freeze to death. That has to be the workings of the Lord with a smile on his face, don't you think?'

Judd nodded, his thoughts far away back home in Red Bluffs. He was barely aware of a distant bird call, when Moses suddenly reached over grabbing his arm, putting a finger to his lips.

'You hear that?' Moses whispered. 'Quail don't call at night. Indians must be coming in. You just sit tight. They know and trust me, but I wonder why they're coming here at this hour? That's a mighty unusual thing for them to do. Must be something pretty important for them to do so.'

'Indians?' Judd's eyes narrowed. Leaning forward he searched out into the darkness.

'Yes, they're part of the Southern Paiutes. Broke off from the main tribe because they wouldn't go on any reservation. They're a little wild and unpredictable, but I've worked at teaching them God's ways when they'll listen, trying to moderate some of their savage ways. This band is led by a brave called Red Jacket.'

'Does it work?'

'Sometimes.'

Moses answered the quail call with one of his own, both men straining to see out into the night. No sound could be heard, no snap of dry twigs, or shuffle of feet. One moment the night in front of the cave was empty and still, the next seven ghostly figures appeared in the pulsing firelight as if by magic. Moses slowly came to his feet, making a sign of the cross towards his silent visitors. Judd saw that their long black hair down to their shoulders was wrapped in a broad red headband just above their eyes. They wore striped cotton shirts adorned with double strings of beads around their necks and some

21

coins. One wore a red jacket. A breach clout served the lower half of their body, stopping at knee-high buckskin boots tied at the tops. Each man also wore a gun belt and sheath knife. Four carried older rifles. All seven had their eyes on Judd.

Moses beckoned them to come closer to the fire, explaining Judd's suspicious presence in pigeon English. He raised his hand for a moment, saying something before disappearing back into the cave. Returning, he gave each Indian a small handful of tobacco. 'I sometimes smoke a pipe,' he commented to Judd, 'but I keep tobacco mostly for them. It's an important sign of friendship, for one man to share his tobacco with others. Here, you give them some, too. It will relax them about you being here. They've never seen another white man here at my place.'

The Indians sat exchanging tobacco, lighting hand-made cigarettes from the firepit. But the talk that followed between Moses and the Paiutes didn't take long to turn serious. Even Judd could see their conversation was disturbed, although he couldn't understand a single word of it. When the Indians had finished they got to their feet and had a last few words with Moses, before one more parting glance at Judd. In a moment they disappeared back into the night as silently as they'd come.

'What was that all about?' Judd asked.

'Nothing good. From what they said it sounds like a bunch of outlaw riders rode into Dry Wells and took over the place. They shot it up and took what they wanted, but haven't left town yet. Looks like they might mean to stay for a while. Could be a bunch of Comancheros. They operate on both sides of the border in Mexico, and up here, too. They're godless killers, for sure. And now they show up just when I needed to go into town for supplies!'

'Don't let them stop you. If you need some goods we'll go in together and get what you want. Don't worry about it.'

'Don't worry about it?' Moses leaned closer, trying to decide if Judd was just kidding or not. Miller's expression didn't change.

'That's what I said. We don't have to go in looking for trouble. Why should we hide out here or wait until they leave? What if they stayed in town a week or more, or even a month? You'd still need your supplies. I say we get what you need and take care of it.'

Moses rubbed the back of his neck, pursing his lips as Judd's words sunk in. He tried one more time to explain the danger.

'You do understand, these men, if they are Comancheros, are wanton killers. They think nothing of shooting down anyone who gets in their way. They even kidnap young women and sell them off down in Mexico to the highest bidder. They're the worst of the worst. There's not a shred of human decency in any of them. And you want just you and me to ride in there and pretend like we're not in danger?'

'Yes, I understand what you're saying. But that doesn't change things. You believe in that bible of yours to protect you, and I believe in this six-gun of

23

mine. You've said the Good Book has power over all men, didn't you? With your bible and my pistol, we shouldn't fear much, should we?'

Moses stood dumbstruck at Judd's simple statement of trust. He also knew it was an unspoken challenge, too, his six-gun against Moses' God. The preacher pulled at his chin, struggling for an answer. After a long silence he finally spoke.

'All right . . . by God, we'll go in together, in the morning!'

The half-breed leader of the Comancheros, Rio Kelly, had the dark swarthy skin of his Mexican father, but green eyes from his green-eyed white mother. He was sitting on the porch in front of one of the stores he and his men had cleaned out, in a tilt-back chair, both feet propped up on a porch post. His fancy knee-high boots carried cruel, star-spiked spurs to dig deep into his horse's sides when he wanted more speed. Several of his men lounged up and down the street counting what they'd stolen, or drinking from bottles taken from Dry Wells' one and only saloon.

'Hey Rio!' Indian Bob, one of his men, called out while crossing the street towards him. 'Let's get out of this hick town. There's nothing left to take. Why don't we ride for the border and Juarez? Maybe we find some *señoritas* too, huh?'

Bob's long straight hair hung down to his shoulders, under a flat-brimmed black hat with three eagle feathers stuck in the band. His face and shoulders were scarred with tattoos of Indian symbols. He wore a buckskin vest with no shirt, and striped pants tucked into knee-high moccasin boots tied by thongs at the top. Two pistols were stuck in his cartridge belt without holsters.

Bob was right. Rio was just about ready to get up and prepare to leave, when he saw a smudge of dust still far out of town but coming closer. He raised his hand. 'Wait a minute. We might not be done yet.' He stared until he was certain it was a wagon coming closer.

Moses was at the reins, while Judd sat next to him, his rifle out of sight under the spring seat under a blanket. The look on Moses' face said that he was already suffering second thoughts about coming into Dry Wells. As the wagon drew closer, both men could see horses at hitching posts along the street, and men along the boardwalks watching them come in.

'Looks like there's a pretty big bunch of them,' Moses warned under his breath.

'Yeah, there's a few. Head right for Dennison's. Isn't that where you said you wanted to go?'

As the wagon made its way down the street, each man came to his feet following it, until a line of the grimy-looking killers came to a stop in front of Everett Dennison's store. Rio Kelly got to his feet, standing with both hands on his gun belt. He eyed the pair of wagon men as the Comancheros gathered around the wagon waiting for Moses and Judd to get down. Miller looked up, seeing Rio's bandoliers of bullets forming an X across his chest. A pair of fancy pearl-handled revolvers were snug in their holsters. Kelly read the religious sign on the side of the wagon, and it brought a wicked smile to his face. He decided to have some fun before stripping the two men of anything valuable, including the wagon.

'Hey preacher . . . you know how to say your prayers?' He made the remark as sarcastically as possible so his men could hear it.

'I do,' Moses answered, trying not to sound intimidated by the insult, 'and I also know the Good Lord protects me from all evil. It's a lesson you and this rabble you have with you, should learn, whatever your name is.'

The smile on Rio's face suddenly disappeared. He didn't like being bested in front of his men, but he decided to play the game just a bit longer, before he killed both men.

'Hey you,' he nodded at Judd, 'you a bible thumper too, like this fool?'

'No,' Judd slowly shook his head. 'I can't say that I am, but there might be something to it. My friend here certainly thinks so.'

'Do you think he still would if I put my pistol to the back of his head, and told him to throw that worthless book in the dirt, and that he had five seconds left to live?'

'I don't know, but what kind of coward would gun down an unarmed man, without giving him a chance?'

'A chance? You think this skinny bag of bones has any chance against me, Rio Kelly?'

'Maybe not, but I would. You want to try me?'

A smile came back over Rio's face, and his men laughed, at the same time waiting for their boss to answer. Only a fool ready to die would challenge Rio like that. His reputation with a six-gun was known far and wide. Some cowboy sitting in a wagon didn't have a hoot and holler in hell of going up against him. He decided to play with Miller for a few moments longer before killing him.

'OK, you have a pistol, and a big mouth to go with it. Get down out of that wagon, and I'll kill you first, so my men don't have to pull your body off the seat. Then I'll kill the scarecrow.'

'Just one more thing. You tell your men to stay out of it,' Judd bargained.

'They won't need to help me. They can pick up what's left of you when I'm done.'

Judd turned to start down, his eyes briefly on Moses, before silently nodding at the rifle under the seat. Moses's eyes widened at the inference, but he said nothing. Rio walked out into the middle of the street, lifting both pistols slightly in their holster to make a quick draw. Judd stopped thirty feet away, turning to face the Comanchero leader, while Rio's men crowded around the back of the wagon to see the fun. Rio spread his feet slightly for even balance, calling out.

'You ready to die, cowboy?'

'Make your play!'

Rio's hands slapped for both pearl-handled pistols. Gripping big iron he started them up. Both barrels had just cleared holsters, but Judd's lightning fast cross-draw had his .45 already levelled up. One thundering shot cut into Rio, spinning him to the ground. He tried desperately to crawl a few feet before collapsing, both pistols still clutched in his hands, a thin stream of bright red blood running down the side of his mouth. Rio Kelly's days of killing and marauding were over.

For one split second Rio's men stood open-mouthed, frozen in disbelief, before Indian Bob screamed, 'Kill him!'

Judd spun on the men, continuing to fire, killing Bob first as the rest struggled to pull their weapons. Two more Comancheros went down before the sudden roar of rifle fire behind them cut down three more, Moses standing on the wagon seat and firing Judd's rifle as fast as he could work the lever. In ten seconds it was all over. Dead and dying men lay in the street, the remaining men dropping their pistols, throwing up their hands, caught in the murderous fire.

Suddenly up and down the street store owners ran out on to the boardwalk, shouting in relief at the death of the killers. Judd ran to the wagon and took the rifle from Moses' hands as he collapsed back down on the seat, shaking like a leaf in a wind storm, dropping his head into both hands. Every savage instinct he'd taught himself to abhor and had preached against to others for years, he'd forgotten in one violent moment of savage killing. 'No . . . no . . . no . . .' he moaned over and over again.

Judd saw his friend in misery, but moved quickly, levelling the rifle on the remaining Comancheros. 'Leave your pistols right on the ground and pick up the body of your boss and the others, and get them on a horse and away from here. And don't any of you ever come back here again, you understand!'

A group of store owners converged on Judd and Moses, shouting their congratulations, pounding Judd on the back, as everyone tried talking at the same time. Behind them Rio's body was being lifted on his horse, belly down and roped in place, until the last of the gang saddled up, pulling their dead behind them, riding down the street out of town at a gallop.

'I never thought I'd ever see anything like what you two men just did,' one of the store owners said. 'I thought they'd kill us all!'

'Me too,' another man added. 'They just about cleaned out everything I had, but I'd've gladly paid it all to see that Rio dead, and his men run out of town.'

'Say, what about you, mister, we all know Moses, but none of us ever saw you before – you got a name?'

'It's Judd Miller, but it doesn't make any difference. I was just passing through. I might stay a little longer now, try to help Moses get himself back together after all this. I'm used to it, but he's not.' He looked over at Moses still sitting in shock, staring at the floorboards of his wagon. 'Right now I think I'd better get him out of here, away from all this.'

29

CHAPTER THREE

The welcoming coolness of Moses' cave after the long hot ride back under a blistering sun did little to help Moses' deep depression about what he'd done in Dry Wells. He said almost nothing on the wagon ride, and Judd didn't push a conversation. Sudden gunplay and killing in that way can have an unpredictable way of affecting each man involved in it, especially when it happens so unexpectedly. Moses was struggling mightily with himself, that was plain to see. Once inside, Judd poured two tin cups of cold water, handing Moses one, before draining his own dry.

'Feel a little bit better?' He finally asked, looking up at Moses as he sat with a forlorn expression on his face.

'No . . . no, I don't,' he slowly shook his head. 'How can I feel better about a killing I had a hand in, after all these years I've preached against it? I picked up that rifle and started firing just like it was second nature to me. How in God's name could I have done something like that?'

'I know it's not easy for you, but let me ask you something. Tell me what you think would have happened if you hadn't helped me when I needed it most? I had three shots left in my six-gun. There were more Comancheros than that. I'd say there's a pretty good chance I wouldn't be standing here asking you about all this. I would likely have been cut down and roped over my horse, just like Rio Kelly was. Yes, you broke a vow not to be a part of violence, but in doing so you saved my life, and probably yours, too. Think about that Moses, because there's a whole lot of truth in it. The Good Book you live by says, "an eye for an eye, a tooth for a tooth". So what do you think it means? I think it means exactly what it says, and that's what you did.'

Moses stared back letting his words sink in before responding. 'It also says to "turn the other cheek".'

'Yes it does, but not when you're facing six guns trying to kill us. The fact is, you picking up that rifle, and by using it, you saved my life and yours too. I owe you one for it.'

Moses didn't answer this time. He knew Judd's point was a powerful one that could not be denied, but still he had to have his say: 'You owe me nothing, Judd. All I did was react like I might have back in my bad old days. I just don't know why I did!'

'Well, I'm glad you did. I imagine you'll have to try and answer that for yourself – but remember you also did your friends in Dry Wells a lot of good, too. You saved them from going through even more fear and

31

misery at the hands of Rio and his men. And that doesn't count a lot of other folks who would have been killed or robbed, if Rio and his men had rode out of town going on to someplace else. Think about it, and don't be too hard on yourself.'

Miller stayed with the preacher for another week, helping him fight off his depression, before deciding it was time that he moved on. When he announced his intentions, Moses was saddened and surprised to hear it.

'Why leave, where would you go? Why don't you stay here a while longer? We make a pretty good team, don't you think? You could even ride with me in the wagon, while I try to get back to my ministering.'

'I could, but the odd thing is I'm getting too comfortable being here. When that happens it means it's time to saddle up. Something might be coming to catch up to me, know what I mean?'

'No, not exactly. You're in the middle of the desert. Where would you go?'

'What's over those mountains beyond Dry Wells?'

'I'm not sure. I've never gone that far – and you've never really told me what you're running from, either. You know a lot about me, but I really don't know that much about you, except for the few things you've said. If you mean to pull out, I'd at least like to know why you're always on the run?'

Judd stared hard at the preacher. He knew Moses was curious, and that he probably did owe him at least that much of an explanation. A small smile came over his face at Moses' boldness in asking him.

'I'll just say this much. A little over a month ago my brother and I were starting to build a small ranch north of here before he was murdered by the same people who came to do the same thing to me. I had to shoot my way out, and I've been on the run ever since. There's a lot more to it, and most of it I still don't even know about. But one thing I am sure of is that if it takes me a lifetime to find out who was behind it, I will.'

'I see,' Moses shook his head. 'You know, you don't have to run any more. No one is going to find you out here. Stay a while longer. You'll see I'm right.'

'Somehow the past has a way of catching up to you, if you stay too long in once place. Word of those killings in town will get around – it's just a matter of time. Someone will come looking, asking questions. You've been a good friend when I needed one most, but I'm going to pack up and leave in the morning. If I stay it will only bring trouble here, sooner or later. Take my word for it. Trouble travels faster than the wind.'

Moses sat dejected, chin resting on both hands, looking back at Judd. He let out a long sigh of regret before speaking again. 'All right, if that's the way you want it, I guess I can't change your mind. At least be sure and take enough grub to keep you going for a while. No telling when you'll find someplace else again where you can buy some.'

The first piercing rays of the morning sun bit into

the desert, scorching everything it touched, as Judd tightened the saddle cinch on his horse, preparing to leave. Moses came out of the cave with Judd's saddle-bags filled to the top.

'You've got both water bags topped off?' he asked.

'I have. And I took one long pull myself. I don't expect to find anything like you have here anytime soon.'

'No, it's not likely, unless the Good Lord is going to ride with you, like he did me.' He tried one last time: 'You ought to stay a while longer. You know that, don't you?'

Judd didn't answer, securing the saddle-bags in place. Finished, he turned back to the tall man, sticking out his hand, both locking in solid grips, eyes levelled on each other.

'Thanks for everything, Moses. You've been a real friend when I needed one the most.'

'No, thank you, Judd. You saved me when I thought I'd lost my way. I only hope everything goes well for you wherever you go. Stay safe. I'll pray for you. I know God will be looking out for you.'

'Then I know I'll be all right.' He flashed a quick smile.

Judd mounted up, starting away, looking back one last time with a quick wave, while Moses quietly whispered a prayer to himself.

'Take care of him, Lord. I know he's going to need you now more than ever.'

Judd reached the quiet, dusty streets of Dry Wells

later that morning, riding straight through town as store owners and their few customers gawked behind windows, watching him pass, talking in whispers. Any man who could handle a six-gun like that had to be dangerous, even if he had saved the town from the Comancheros only days earlier. Reaching the last building short of leaving, the figure of a man crossed the street in front of him. Miller reined to a halt.

'Can you tell me where this wagon road leads to up in those mountains?' He nodded toward the foreboding high country ahead.

The old man squinted up at him, shading his eyes with one hand. 'No place that most decent folks want to go, that's for sure.'

'Why is that?'

'Because it's a lawless hell hole, that's why!'

'Does it have a name?'

'Yup. It's called Hang Town, and it's earned every single letter in it up there in them Wolf Fang mountains.'

'Hang Town, huh? You know how far it is from here?'

'I'm told it's about a one-week ride. Never been there myself, and hope I never do. It's one of those places you're either quick or dead. Which one are you, mister?'

Judd didn't answer. Instead he thanked the old-timer, preparing to start away.

'You don't mean to ride up in there, after what I said, do ya?'

'Yes, it looks like I am.'

35

The man shook his head, grunting. 'You don't listen very good, but it's your neck, not mine. Everyone here in town saw your gunplay. Up there might be a different story. I guess you'll have to figure that out for yourself . . . if you live long enough. Good luck. You're gonna' need it!'

Judd tipped his hat, urging the big bay away until Dry Wells slowly grew smaller behind him until the buildings became distorted shapes dancing in shimmering waves of morning heat.

Over the next five days he ascended the long, slow climb into the Wolf Fang mountains, leaving the desert lowlands spread out below in patterns of endless dry gullies and arroyos, twisting away like so many tan spider webs. As he gained height, the blistering heat changed to cooler nights, the clouds driven by dark winds that made Judd shiver under his thin wool blanket. By dawn on the sixth day, the rocky wagon road he'd been following made a final, sharp S turn and headed for the last ridges close along the skyline. He began to wonder if all the talk of a town up here in this remote and isolated range held any truth, whether it existed at all. He'd not seen one sign of any living thing since leaving Dry Wells. Maybe it was just another ghost town, one of those that suddenly sprang to life and which died just as quickly, like so many others, founded on wild hope before being abandoned in the realization that in reality there was none.

Judd spurred his horse the last few yards, reining

to a halt on the final knife-edged ridge, looking down the steep drop on the other side. Instantly he heard the distant thud of far-away gunshots echoing back and forth, off canyon walls. Urging the horse farther down the ridge, he could just make out a tiny cluster of buildings far below tucked away in a hidden side canyon. Hang Town hadn't died: those gunshots meant it still breathed life – but what kind?

Miller started down the steep, rocky trail as the town steadily grew closer. Half an hour later he could finally see grey, weathered wooden buildings mixed with some erected out of dark natural stone, along a crowded street. Rounding the last bend leading into town, he pulled to a stop at a tall, dead pine. A faded, hand-painted sign had just two words on it: HANG TOWN. Below, a short length of rope tied in a hangman's knot was nailed to the sign. Judd sat in the saddle a moment before urging his horse ahead into the first buildings. The sight and sound of shouts, gunshots and the pounding hoofs of galloping horses revealed three riders racing down the street, firing pistols over their heads, while a crowd of men on the sidelines cheered them on for greater speed and recklessness.

Judd eased out of the saddle, tied his horse at a hitching post, then stood next to a crowd of rough-looking men anxiously watching the riders as they approached the far end of town through a rising cloud of dust. The instant they reached the end of the street they yanked their horses around and started back up it again, whipping and digging spurs into their flanks.

'Come on Sloat, give 'em hell!' the man next to Judd yelled, rooting for the rider in the lead, as the racers came thundering closer, while he tried making more side bets. 'I got fifty more says Sloat wins. What about you, mister, you want some of it?' He turned to Miller, waving a fistful of dollars in his face.

'I'm new in town,' Judd shook his head, with the quick excuse, 'I don't know who's riding what, so I'm not in the bet.'

Robbie Wheller quickly turned away, looking for someone else, as the horses flashed by and Judd saw the man riding in the lead, Cayce Sloat, whipping his horse savagely with a short leather quirt. Cayce would stand out in any crowd, mounted or not. He was a big man physically, wearing heavy leather chaps lined along the edges with flashing silver conchos. His striped, brightly coloured shirt was worn under a fuzzy, white wool vest. His black pants and boots set off the same mop of unruly hair worn under a wide-brimmed hat to match. On his side a long-barrelled pistol jostled up and down in its holster at every leap of his horse.

'You got 'em Sloat, don't slow down now!' Wheller shouted at his hero as the horses flashed by open mouthed, for one last run down and back. 'Ain't no one going to outride Cayce. I don't care who tries it!' He excitedly elbowed Judd in the ribs. 'When he's ridin' like this, both me and him make money!'

As the trio of riders turned, starting back, one of the other riders pulled up almost even with Sloat, challenging him for the lead, threatening his victory. Quick as a rattlesnake strike, Cayce lashed out with his quirt, striking the rider full across the face, opening a bloody welt, causing the man to pull back, staying second. Streaking across the finish line, Cayce rode back to the yelling crowd of men and got down, coming up to Wheller.

'Well, did we make any money?' he roared, a toothy grin spreading across his sweaty, whiskered face.

'We sure did, Cayce. I ain't counted all of it yet, but I'd have to say we had to make maybe . . . two hundred dollars?'

'Two hundred, is that all?'

'Well, yeah, but remember, everyone knows you usually win, so it's hard to get a bet against you. You gotta' know that, don't you?'

Sloat looked around at the crowd of men, quickly noticing a new face he'd never seen before.

'What about you, cowboy?' he pushed out his chin at Miller. 'Did you bet on me to win or lose?' He eyed Judd suspiciously, the men surrounding him leaning closer, waiting for the stranger to answer.

'I didn't do either one. I'm new here. I don't know anyone, or who was racing. I just watched.'

'Just watched, huh? Next time you'll know who to bet on, if you're around here long enough,' he turned back to the knot of men. 'Let's get on down to Rickert's, so I can wash down some of this dust!'

The crowd of men moved off, leaving Judd standing alone in the street, watching them go. The brief encounter with Cayce Sloat was enough for Judd to know he was the big man in Hang Town, and someone to watch out for. Sloat had some lingering suspicions of his own about the new man. He took one long look back over his shoulder, as he and his pals continued down the street for the whiskey house.

If Judd thought his introduction to Hang Town was wild and wide open, once the sun died out behind the rocky heights of the Wolf Fang range, the unbridled raucousness only increased. Coal oil lamps were lit up and down the street, bringing new life into gambling houses and saloons. Laughter, loud shouts and even occasional gunfire permeated the evening air. If a town could survive on whiskey alone, Hang Town was proving that point in spades.

Miller walked the streets, pausing just long enough to look into each establishment before moving on. Most were crowded with players or drinkers. Nearing Rickert's, he stopped, looking over the double doors into the popular watering hole. The big room was a sea of noisy men in motion, wall to wall. Above the endless chin music, Cayce Sloat's booming voice could be heard. He was sitting at a card table near the end of a long bar, playing poker with four other men. Judd knew from his brief encounter earlier, that it was just a matter of time before he and Sloat ended up face to face – he could feel it as certain as sundown. Pushing through the doors, he stepped inside, slowly working his way across the room.

At the poker table Rickert's house dealer, Frank Kincade, had the fancy clothes, poise and look of a middle-aged man who had always made his living dealing off a fresh deck of cards, never breaking a sweat at manual labour. The first tinge of grey hair showed on his long sideburns and moustache. His well tanned face had the first faint lines of crows' feet around the eyes. He'd just won a large pot laying down a red heart flush over Sloat's pair of aces and another player's three of a kind. The fourth man at the table threw in his hand, getting to his feet and shaking his head.

'That's it for me, boys. I'm not contributing any more money to Bart Rickert, the way these cards have been running. You boys can knock heads with Kincade, I'm out.'

The third player said he'd stay for one more hand, then pull out too, if he lost. Cayce yelled over to the bartender to bring him a new bottle of rye whiskey. 'I'm in until I clean you out, Kincade,' he snorted, glaring at the dealer, 'and you better be sure all these cards are coming off the top of the deck, too!' He pulled up his pistol, placing it on the table next to the new bottle.

'You're having a bad run of luck, Cayce. You ought to sit tonight out. Once Lady Luck turns against you, it's best to listen to her,' Kincade suggested.

'You just deal the cards and let me worry about Lady Luck.'

'As you, wish. Everyone ante up ten dollars for the new pot. Anyone else want in to fill this empty chair?'

Kincade turned in his seat, looking at men standing around the table watching the game. Cayce looked up too, spotting Judd standing near the bar.

'Hey you, cowboy, get over here and fill this chair!' he shouted, and everyone turned to see who Sloat was yelling at.

Judd Miller picked up his glass of beer and walked over to the table, never taking his eyes off Cayce. For the first time Sloat noticed Judd carried his six-gun on his left side with the pistol butt forward, even though he drank and carried his glass in his right hand. Reaching the table, the two stared at each other for several uncomfortable seconds until Sloat broke the silence.

'That's a damn strange way to carry a pistol. It's on the wrong side,' he mocked. 'I guess you don't have to use it much. Sit on down here and put some money on the table. We're short one man.'

'I'm not a gambler, at least not at cards.' Judd shook his head, still standing.

'You're not, huh? Looks like you don't gamble on horse races and now cards, either. You aren't going to live much longer around here, being scared of everything. This ain't Chicago, you know. You better figure that out real quick.'

'I've done my share of gambling, and then some.'
'Like what?'
'Like, staying alive.'

Cayce threw his head back, laughing out loud. When he finally stopped, he stared hard at Judd. 'You must think you're a real hard case, huh, cowboy?'

42

'Takes a smart man to know his limits,' Kincade suddenly cut in.

'You stay out of this. No one asked you what you think!'

'That's not what I said,' Judd answered.

'Then what in hell are you talking about?'

Judd stood at the table looking down on Sloat, while the crowd of men who had gathered, silently watching the verbal sparring, wondering how far it would go before Cayce did something about it.

'You gonna sit down, or not?' He finally demanded an answer.

'No. I'm not in this game. Get someone else.'

Sloat wasn't used to anyone standing up to him like this, but there was something in Miller's cool resolve that made him uncertain if he should push it any further, at least for right now. He glanced at Kincade and the other man sitting at the table. Neither said a word. Taking in a long, slow breath, Cayce poured himself another drink. 'If everyone is too scared to sit in, I guess we'll play three-handed. Deal them cards, Kincade.' He shot one more long look at Miller, making it clear who he was talking about.

Back at the bar, Judd was finishing his beer when a man with his hat pulled low over his face looked furtively around the room, before edging closer. He began talking in a low whisper, surprising Judd by his sudden presence.

'You better not mess with Sloat and his bunch, mister. He'd kill you for a lot less than what you just

43

said to him.'

Miller turned, sizing up his uninvited guest. One quick look was all it took to see he appeared nearly destitute. His floppy hat barely hid a thin, unshaven face thick in dark stubble. His jacket, shirt and pants were dusty and frayed at the edges above a pair of boots with soles worn nearly through. Most notice-able of all was his entire outfit. It looked to be an old business suit of some kind.

'Why are you telling me something I already know?' Judd asked.

'Because I saw you when you rode in. I know what happens to strangers who cross Sloat like that.'

'And what's that?'

'They just up and disappear one day. No one ever asks why or where they went.'

'Disappear?'

'Yes, Sloat and his men kill them and get rid of the bodies. Probably down some canyon, where the wolfs can feed on what's left. You're new around here. You don't know how things really are. When you rode in you insulted Sloat by not betting on him. I knew right off there'd be trouble between you two. He's not going to forget that. I know what I'm talking about. You better listen.'

Miller studied the shorter man's tired face and pleading eyes. 'You have a name?'

'I'm Lee Hollis.'

Judd stuck out his hand. 'Judd Miller,' he glanced around the room to be sure no one saw them shake.

'We can't talk in here. You got someplace to stay?'

44

Hollis asked.

'No, not yet. Why do you ask?'

'Because you can't stay in Hang Town. Sloat will find out where you're at and do something about it. I've got an old mining shack several miles from here. If you want, you can stay there for a while. . . .'

'I might take you up on that. I'll finish this beer, and we can get out of here.'

'No, no. Not together. I'll go first, and you wait five minutes, then come out. I'll be a few doors up the street.'

CHAPTER FOUR

The shadowy figures of the two riders left town with Hollis in the lead riding a mule, and Judd behind, under a night sky ablaze with diamond-bright stars that seemed so close they could almost reach out and touch them. The narrow trail started steadily downhill, skirting steep drop-offs against vertical rock walls. A full hour later, Judd began to wonder if his new friend actually had a cabin at all, until Hollis finally pulled to a stop, pointing up a narrow opening in the rocky wall.

'My place is right up here,' he kicked the mule ahead. Minutes later they reined to a halt in front of the shadowy outline of the tin-roofed structure.

'You can unsaddle your horse, and put him out back. There's a small fence to keep my mule in, too.'

Once inside the shack, Hollis lit a coal oil lamp that illuminated the single room. Miller was surprised to see how neat and comfortable everything seemed to be, the exact opposite of his new-found friend. A thick coloured blanket was spread over the single spring bed, alongside a small table covered in a red-and-white checkered oil-skin tablecloth. Plates, glasses, knives and forks were neatly stacked on a shelf along one wall, next to boxes containing all manner of food and supplies. A small, pot-bellied stove sat in the middle of the room with a table nearby. Atop it was a stack of old newspapers, next to a pair of thick leather saddle-bags with the name 'Well's Fargo' etched across their front.

'I've got some coffee, if you'd like a cup?' Lee suggested.

'I won't say I couldn't use it, if you want to make it.'

Hollis fed the pot-bellied stove with kindling until it sprang to life, popping and crackling cheerily, and beginning to warm the ice-cold room. It took only minutes for the coffee pot to begin a boiling hiss.

'This is quite a place you've got for yourself,' Judd said. 'How did you find it?'

'Actually, by accident. Years ago they had word of a gold strike up here, but there isn't an ounce of gold in these volcanic mountains, and they left just as fast as they came. I guess someone took the time to build this old place. I'm sure glad they did. I had a horse and the mule when I first came up here, but the horse broke his leg on a rocky trail and I had to shoot him. Now all I've got is the mule, but he works good enough, probably even better than a horse. More surefooted.'

'How long have you been up here?'

'See that calendar?' Lee pointed to the numbered

47

sheet hanging on the wall. 'I mark off every day, just to keep some kind of record. I've been here a little over eight months. Like most men in Hang Town, I can't go back down into the flats where I used to live. All that's waiting for me down there is a trial and a jail cell. How about you? Everybody up here is running from something. What's your story?'

'It's too complicated to get into. The difference is, I'm going back. I just don't know when, right now.'

'I guess you know that Hang Town is the last stop on the outlaw trail. It's like an armed camp of men all willing to shoot it out with any law that tries coming up here – so they don't. It would take an army to overrun it.'

Judd eyed Hollis thoughtfully before speaking again. 'I wouldn't take you for a bank robber or a hold-up man.'

'I'm not.'

'Then why are you here?'

Lee didn't answer for a moment, thinking over how far he should go explaining anything. After a long pause he rubbed the back of his neck with both hands and began telling his story.

'I used to run a Wells Fargo stage stop down in Tonopah. Just me and a teenage kid to handle the horses when they came in. My wife took sick bad, and the doctor said it was cholera. I needed a good doctor in the city, but didn't have the money to get her there. I handled a lot of cash each week when shipments of money in coins and some gold dust came in. I got so desperate to save her life, I went back after locking up the office one night, and took all the cash I could carry in those two saddle-bags over there. I put Adeline in our buggy and took off as fast as I could. But she died on the trail two days later, in my arms. After that I couldn't go back, so I've been here ever since. I'm not a killer like those men in Hang Town. I never put a gun on anyone. I don't even carry one, now. The crime I committed was done without firing a single shot. Maybe in the eyes of law it's just as bad. I don't know.'

'The "law" can mean a lot of different things to different people, depending on who is wearing the badge. I've seen there's as many crooks with a star pinned on their chests as there are real lawmen. I learned that the hard way, when my brother was murdered by someone like that. He was a decent kid, just beginning to get somewhere in life. I'm not even sure why it happened, but I mean to find out if it's the last thing I ever do. I'm going back to get that answer. Someone is going to pay for what was done, even if I have to kill to get it.'

Lee stared back at Judd, sensing from the determination in his voice that he meant every single word of it.

'I thought for a while about going back to Tonopah, but I couldn't face those people who had put their trust in me. Besides, Wells Fargo never closes a case. Not ever. They'd see to it I was sent to prison. Looks like we're both in a fix, don't it?'

'For now maybe, yes. But that won't last forever. Things can change, and people can too.'

Hollis sipped at his coffee cup, thinking over Judd's remarks. He was already certain his new friend would somehow right the wrongs that had been done to him and his brother. For his own situation, he didn't have the kind of grit it took to change much of anything. It was best he just took what came. Lee Hollis was no hell-for-leather cowboy with vengeance in his heart and a cross-draw six-gun. He wished he was, but wishes were like smoke up a winter chimney.

Since Judd's night-time run from Red Bluffs, Cyrus Toomey had been working hard trying to get the Miller property rights transferred into his name, legal or not. Westin Carlyle, Red Bluffs one and only judge, was leery of Toomey's efforts, even though both men were long-time friends both publicly and privately. The more Toomey demanded a paperwork change, the more Carlyle resisted on the grounds that any legal record change would put him in jeopardy if those records were ever questioned. The good judge had no wish to give up fine clothes, a splendid home and profitable law practice on the side, to end up in a territorial prison for record tampering and outright fraud, friends or not.

'Listen to me, Cyrus. This isn't some simple line change with a name, or crossing a few Ts. These land records are subject to a much broader review, if they're ever brought into question and challenged. And that's especially true if Miller ever shows up here again to challenge them. Both you and I could end up in prison for something like this. Now, if Miller could be proven dead, and he had no other family, that might cast a new light on the whole thing, but not where things stand right now.'

'He's got to be as dead as his brother is. Bass and my posse chased him all the way south of here nearly a hundred miles, clear down to desert country. The whole bunch of them barely made it back alive, that country is so bad. How much more proof do you need than that?'

'What I need is either a body, or a coroner's report, if there's any sort of town to make one in.'

'There isn't any town out there. All it is is rattlesnakes, poison water, and cactus twenty feet tall. It's a no man's land. No one is ever going to find what's left of him, after the coyotes get done. Can't you understand that!'

Carlyle massaged his temples, closing his eyes for a moment as he searched for an answer. After a long silence he looked up with a sigh. 'There might be another way to open this land deed up, if he never returns to claim it. I believe there is a time limit on something like this, until someone is considered dead, and the property can go up for public action, if no family members come forward. I'd have to go to my law books, but I think it takes several years, and a public notice has to be printed in newspapers.'

'I don't have years. The Western Cascade railroad people have already begun making serious inquiries about bringing a new line through here. They want to go even farther west. That Miller property is something they need, to do that. The cost of changing plans to go around it is more than they are willing to spend. I've seen their proposal on their site maps. I've got to have that deed in my name, and I mean in any human way possible, legal or not!'

Judd stayed out of sight at Lee's hidden cabin for the next ten days while Hollis made two trips into Hang Town for food and some supplies. Lee was smart enough to time his arrival right after sundown when long shadows of evening were creeping up canyon walls and he'd be least noticed. The first trip in he went unnoticed, but on the second, two of Sloat's men saw him loading his mule in front of Gant's Feed Store.

'Hey,' Jackson Keller elbowed his pal, 'ain't that the little man who tried to help that cowboy . . . what's his name, Miller?'

'Yeah, sure looks like him, all right. Cayce's been asking about the both of them, too.'

'He sure has. We better tell him about this. Let's move while he's still in town. Sloat will want to have a little talk with him, for sure.'

Cayce Sloat rushed out of Rickert's with Keller and Harper at his side. 'Where did you see that little rat?'

'Up by the feed store.' Keller pointed up the street into darkening shadows.

'C'mon. I don't want him to get out of town before I get my hands on him!'

The three men ran up the street until they reached Gant's. 'Where is he?' Sloat demanded, turning to look up and down the street. 'You two sure it was him?'

'Yeah, I'm sure. Who else rides a mule into town?' Jackson snickered, side-eying his boss.

'I'll run up the street and look around the corner,' Harper volunteered, taking off with his chaps slapping at his legs. 'He can't be very far away!'

Reaching the corner he saw Hollis up ahead just starting down the trail heading out of town. 'Hey you, hold up a minute!' he shouted, without breaking stride. Lee looked back, instantly fearful anyone could recognize him. Instead of stopping, he urged his mule ahead, kicking it in the ribs to make it go faster. Harper saw he was trying to get away and quickly pulled his pistol, firing a sudden shot over Lee's head, forcing him to pull to a halt. Catching up with the little man, he yanked the reins out of his hands.

'Someone wants to have a talk with you,' he fought to catch his breath. 'And don't you try . . . to run away from me again.'

'I gotta' get on home. It's already dark.' Hollis protested.

'You ain't "gotta" do anything, but what you're told. Sloat wants to talk to you.'

'I've got nothing to say to him.'

'That's what you think. C'mon. He's waiting for you. If you're smart, you'll answer anything he asks you.'

Harper led the mule back into town where Cayce and Killer were leaning on a hitching rail, waiting for them. 'Get down,' Cayce ordered, grabbing Lee by his jacket collar, roughly pulling him out of the saddle. 'I been hearing that cowboy pal of yours might be staying at your place. Is that so?'

Lee's eyes widened, staring up at Sloat without blinking. For a few agonizing seconds he was too scared to answer. Sloat shook him like a rag doll, demanding he answer him: 'Talk, or I'll beat it out of you!' he threatened.

Lee swallowed hard, Cayce's strong, whiskey breath nauseating him, as the big man pulled him even closer. 'I don't know . . . nothing about him.' He finally got the words out, trying to pull back.

'You don't, huh? I say you do, and there's going to be hell to pay if you don't start talking. Where's this shack you live in? I'll go there and look for myself. And you're coming with me.'

Hollis was trapped, and knew it. Maybe he could still lie his way out of it. 'He only stayed with me a couple days, and then rode out.' He tried an alibi, praying it would work.

'Rode out to where?'

'He didn't say. He just said it was time to move on, and left.'

'You're a yellow liar!' Cayce pulled up his six-gun and swung it down hard across Lee's head, knocking him to his knees; the gash instantly started bleeding profusely, soaking the matted hair under his hat. Before Lee could catch his breath from the sudden blow, Sloat kicked him hard in the ribs, doubling him over on the ground, leaving him struggling to catch his breath. 'I said, where is this shack of yours, and this time I better get an answer, or I'll give you some more of this!'

Hollis slowly rolled over, face up, gasping for breath, the three men standing over him looking down. 'Have . . . mercy . . . Sloat. I don't know . . . nothing more.' His voice was barely a whisper.

'Have mercy?' Sloat laughed out loud, booting him in the ribs again. 'You either tell me or I'll kick you to death, right here in the street. And no one is going to try to help you, either. Now spit it out!'

Keller began to wince as the beating grew worse, until even he thought his boss meant to kill the little man right where he lay. 'Hey, Cayce, I think I might know where that cabin of his is,' he reached over, grabbing Sloat by the shoulder. 'There's a little side canyon about a mile down the trail out of town, where someone told me they did some mining years ago. I'll bet that's it. If you keep kicking him, Harper and me will have to drag his carcass out of town someplace and bury him. Why don't we ride down there and have a look-see for ourselves? Why wear your boots out on him?'

Sloat was sweating, breathing heavily from all the exertion. He stopped, grabbing the hitching rail for support, trying to regain his breath. Looking down on Hollis, he gave him one last boot in the ribs, before straightening up again.

'All right. We'll do that, after I've had a drink, and caught my breath. There's something about that cowboy I didn't like from the start. He could be a bounty hunter, or maybe even a lawman in disguise.

The sooner I take care of him, the better. Let's go.'

'What about him?' Harper looked down on Hollis, rolled up in a ball moaning pitifully.

'Let the little rat lay there!' Sloat wiped his sweaty face with the back of his shirt sleeve. 'He ain't going anyplace for a while. Hell, he might never get up at all!' His sinister laugh echoed up and down the darkened street.

Lee Hollis lay in the dark a long time before trying to move. When he did, his broken body was racked in pain, but he stayed conscious. He knew he had to get back to his shack and Judd Miller before Sloat and his men did. Slowly, groaning with each effort, he managed to roll over and grab the hitching rail, then struggled to pull himself up, inch by inch, fighting back the urge to cry out. He could hear the bones in his broken ribs crunch as he did so, making each breath a knife stab of pain; finally he staggered upright, hanging on to the hitching rail with both hands to keep from collapsing. He reached for the reins on his mule. Pulling it closer he grabbed the saddle horn, mustering his last ounce of strength to pull his broken body up into the saddle. Then he started away back down the trail.

Judd had begun to wonder what was taking Hollis so long to ride back from Hang Town. He stepped outside the door into the chilly air of the night, peering up the shadowy trail leading in. At first he saw nothing, but then he thought he heard the first faint sounds of distant hoofbeats coming closer. 'Lee, is that you?' he called out – but there was no answer.

His hand went down and pulled up the six-gun. If it wasn't Lee, it could only mean trouble was riding in. He stepped back around the corner of the small shack where he could still see the dim trail, but not be seen. The shadowy outline of Lee's mule came into view, but the image didn't look right. Judd moved back out walking quickly closer. That's when he realized Hollis was draped over the animals' neck, hanging on, moaning low under his breath.

'Lee, what happened, are you hurt? Here, let me help you down.' Judd ran to him.

'No . . . no, don't. I'll try to do it myself. My ribs are caved in. If you grab me . . . I'll pass out.'

Lee agonizingly slid down off the saddle, grabbing Judd by the shoulder, begging him to keep him upright until he could get inside the cabin. Once there he collapsed on the bed, face up. Miller quickly lit the coal oil lamp, coming to his side for his first real look at the little man. His face was battered, dirty and bloody, creased with pain, streaked with tears.

'Who did this to you?' Judd demanded, beginning to clean his face.

'Sloat . . . and some of his men . . . tried to get me . . . to tell them where you were . . . out here.'

'Why didn't you, instead of taking a beating like this? I can take care of Sloat and anyone who hangs around him.'

'You . . . don't understand, Judd. He means to . . . come here and kill you.'

'Are you sure they're coming here?'

'Yeah . . . I am.'

'I'm going to try and clean you up, then wrap those ribs of yours. You just lay still, while I get a few things. I'm no doctor, but I'll do the best I can. Do you own a weapon of any kind?'

'I've got . . . an old pistol, over there in that box.'

'Is it loaded?'

'I don't know . . . I don't think so. I haven't fired a shot with it in years.'

Judd retrieved the ancient weapon, which broke open from the top for reloading.

It was empty. He rummaged around further in the box until finding a box of bullets for the little .22 caliber pistol. Loading it he came back to the bedside.

'If Sloat does show up and gets past me, you use this, you understand?'

Lee looked up, a thin stream of bright red blood running down the side of his mouth. He started to answer, but only nodded yes. Judd looked around the shack for something to wrap his ribs in. Tearing up an old bed sheet, he carefully wrapped Lee's body without making it too tight. When done, he spoke again.

'I'm going outside, in case anyone followed you here. You just rest as easy as you can. I'll put the water jug and a glass next to you in case you want a drink. I'll snuff out the lamp too, for now.'

Judd grabbed his rifle leaning next to the door. Stepping back outside into the icy breath of night air, he bristled at the savage beating the little man had endured at the hands of Cayce Sloat, vowing to make him pay for what he'd done. Men like Sloat didn't deserve to live. Once again Judd found himself ready to use his six-gun to do something about it. Only months earlier, he and his brother were working to make their new ranch a paying proposition, and now everything had changed to showdowns and killing gunfights, with a price on his own head. It seemed almost unreal that any of this could have happened. He took in a deep breath, closing his eyes for a moment, before walking a short distance away stopping at a bend in the narrow trail where he could see a short distance ahead. He listened intently but heard nothing.

With no moon, stars cast a ghostly glow over everything, turning dark shadows into lurking gunmen ready to leap up and open fire. He studied each and every one until the sound of slow walked hoof beats invaded the silence of night. Judd lifted the rifle, aiming through a narrow gap in the rocky wall, waiting for horsemen to fill it. The instant the first figure did, he shouted a sudden challenge.

'Let those reins drop, and throw up your hands!'

The reaction was instant. Thunderous pistol fire echoed off rock walls as all three riders opened fire, and bullets ricochet off stony walls, and they struggled to climb back in the saddle, fighting to turn their horses around in the narrow passageway. Judd worked the lever action rifle as fast as he could, until one of the men screamed out in pain. In a matter of seconds the deadly confrontation was over, the sound of running horses fading away. Judd's bullets had found their mark on at least one man. But which one?

CHAPTER FIVE

Back inside the shack, Judd relit the kerosene lamp, quickly crossing the room to where Lee lay. Lowering the lamp, he began talking explaining what had happened outside, but stopped in mid sentence. A closer look at Lee's bloody face and his clouded, half-opened eyes told him that Lee had heard none of it, or ever would again. Judd put a finger to the side of the little man's neck. There was no pulse. The savage beating he'd suffered at the hands of Cayce Sloat had killed Lee Hollis as surely as a gunshot to the head.

That cold and starry night, Judd buried his friend further up canyon in a shallow grave under a pile of rocks. Returning to the shack, he reloaded the rifle and checked his six-gun to be certain all six cylinders were filled with the grey, round-nosed bullets. He made a vow at that moment to saddle up and ride for Hang Town. Cayce Sloat had a visitor coming, and one who meant to take vengeance on him for what he'd done, or anyone else who got in the way.

Hang Town's street was still lit by the soft glow of

lamplight from inside saloons and gambling houses, when Judd reached the edge of town. Reining to a stop, he took in the scene, hearing voices and muffled laughter drifting up the street. It was just another night of wide-open partying, gambling and drinking – but not to Miller. He meant to turn it into a night of flaming six-guns and a dead man lying in the street – and when he did, he'd be on the run again. Urging his horse ahead, Judd started down the street, heading for Rickert's saloon, where Sloat always hung out.

Reaching the lively watering hole, he eased down out of the saddle, tying his horse to the hitching rail one door up from the popular bar. He wanted the street clear for what was coming. Stepping on to the boardwalk, he looked through the open double doors inside, searching the crowded room for Sloat. Sloat's loud, booming voice quickly identified him, standing at the far end of the bar. As usual, a crowd of admirers gathered around him while he raved on about the cowboy stranger who'd showed up in town only weeks earlier, and had now killed one of his men, Jackson Keller, that very same evening in a night-time ambush outside town. He harangued everyone, wildly waving his hands over his head, about how they should gather up riders and a rope, to go find the killer and hang him. Shouts of support rose up from his excited listeners in the smoke-filled room, until Judd suddenly pushed through the door and everyone turned seeing him. A sudden quiet settled over the room.

'You're a bald-faced liar and a yellow coward!' Miller called out. 'You beat Lee Hollis to death right out here on this street tonight, and now you better step outside and pay for it. If you don't, I'll come back in here and drag you out!' Judd backed out the doors, while the bar-room exploded in excited talk; Cayce looked around for Dave Harper, who quickly pushed his way through the throng of men up to his boss.

'Quick, you get out the side door into the alley, where you can see the street.' Sloat ordered. 'When I get outside, we'll have him in crossfire, before he knows what hit him!'

'Go get 'em, Cayce!' one man standing nearby shouted encouragement.

'Yeah, give him all six shots!' another seconded, as Sloat dramatically tossed down a shot of whiskey, slamming the stubby glass down on the bar for emphasis, before taking up his gunbelt a notch, eyeing the crowd around him with a forced smile.

Sloat couldn't show it, but he wasn't as sure about the showdown waiting for him as his admirers. He'd never been called out face to face before, especially by someone he didn't know, and in front of friends to boot. He worried if he was fast enough to out-pull this bold cowboy waiting for him, or not.

Cayce stepped for the door, pushing through it and out on to the boardwalk. He could just make out Miller's shadowy form standing in the middle of the street forty feet away. A quick glance at the alley to his right, meant Harper was there waiting, even though

63

he couldn't see him. Nothing like an ace in the hole, Cayce thought as he stepped on to the street facing Judd.

'OK, cowboy, you shot off your big mouth. Now let's see just how fast you think you really are!' Sloat shouted, coming to a stop planting his feet slightly apart, steadying himself, right hand poised over his pistol.

At the same instant, Judd caught the dull flash of a pistol barrel slowly emerging from the alley, lit by soft light from inside Rickert's. He spun left on his feet, firing three thundering shots into the darkened passageway. The mortal screams of Dave Harper faded away, along with echoing shots. He went down without ever pulling the trigger. Cayce hesitated for a split second, wide-eyed at seeing his ace in the hole so suddenly dead. He yanked up his big iron, firing at Judd at the same time as Miller turned back crouching, firing his remaining three shots into the big man. Sloat's mouth fell open as the bullets hit. He staggered back, still holding on to his pistol, trying to stay on his feet. A bloody cough welled up in his throat, before he sagged to the ground in slow motion, lying face up on his back. The vicious Hang Town bully was dying on the same street where he'd killed other men.

The crowd of men peeking out around the door at Rickert's pushed cautiously out on to the boardwalk before one man ran for the alley, while others slowly advanced on Sloat's body spread-eagled in the middle of the street, staring down at their hero.

64

'Harper's dead too!' the alley man called out.

'That cowboy killed both of them!' Someone in the knot of men screamed at the top of his lungs, pointing at Judd, who now held an empty six-gun in his hand.

'Let's get that rope and hang him!' Another shouted.

'His pistol is empty. He's fired all six shots. Take him!' A third vigilante incited his pals to action.

Judd ran for this horse. Yanking the Winchester rifle out of its scabbard, he levelled it on the advancing crowd, firing one shot over their heads. The men ducked. Some dropped to their knees, covering their faces with their arms.

'I've got fifteen more shots in this magazine. Who wants to be first to get one in the belly, like Sloat did?' Judd threatened, pushing his foot into the stirrup, and pulling himself up into the saddle with one hand. For the first time he felt the white-hot sting of pain in his side: one of Sloat's bullets had nearly found its mark. He struggled, kicking his horse down the street into the night, while a wild volley of shots was fired after him.

Reaching the little mining cabin, Miller lit the lantern. Taking off his bloody shirt, he examined the open gash that was the bullet wound in his side. He couldn't keep riding with something like this – he'd likely bleed to death. Looking round the room he found a needle and thread in a small drawer. Before threading it, he poured a generous splash of whiskey on the wound, from a bottle Lee kept under his bed.

That liquid fire matched the pain of the wound. Stitch by excruciating stitch he slowly began closing the wound, moaning low each time the needle pierced his flesh, his face twisted in pain as he completed each torturous circle. Sweat rolled down his face, and the pain became so intense he thought he might pass out, but the possibility that the men from the town might know the cabin's location and ride in, kept his adrenalin flowing, forcing him to stay conscious.

Once he had finished the grisly doctoring, he looked around the cabin, gathering up what few items he could, especially the food Lee had brought in from town. He filled a cloth sack and his saddlebags with everything, then hurried outside and tied it all on to his horse.

Judd knew he couldn't ride back through town. Instead he decided the only way left was to head down out of the mountains to whatever might lie ahead. Some while later he looked back and could see the flickering light of many torches dancing in the night, held high by riders turning into the narrow passage leading to the shack. He'd only beaten the hangman's rope by a whisker, without adding his own name to the men who had given Hang Town its fearsome reputation.

Two days after fleeing the night-time shack, Judd Miller found himself far from the mountains, riding through rough hill country covered in sagebrush and gramma grass. With every move he made in the saddle the wound in his side burned as if he were being jabbed with a white hot poker. He kept gingerly surveying the bloodstain on the side of his shirt, knowing he was still bleeding. He needed medical help, but out here in the middle of nowhere that wasn't going to happen. Finally near sundown on the second day he pulled his horse to a halt, and eased himself down out of the saddle. The last rays of sunlight painted the empty land in stark contrasts of shadow and light. Nothing stirred. The land seemed empty, devoid of any living thing. For the first time he felt sick to his stomach, and was beginning to suffer bouts of dizziness.

The narrow ravine he found himself in was lined with low, tough cedars. Pulling a blanket from his saddle pack, he spread it on the ground and sat down, and tried to eat a few bites of hardtack. It didn't help. Giving that up, he lay down and closed his eyes. The last thought he had before falling into an exhausted sleep, was to wonder if he would ever wake up again.

The sun rose the following morning, marching its timeless path slowly across the sky, finally to sink out of sight behind the mountains at sunset. Judd Miller did not stir. A second dawn lit the land. Judd tried opening his eyes, vaguely aware of a voice that seemed far away, and someone's hand brushing his matted hair from his face.

'Hey, mister – you dead or alive?'

He forced his eyes open, and could just make out the fuzzy image of someone leaning close over him, wearing a beat-up cowboy hat, with a curly mop of brown hair nearly as wide as the hat. His eyes cleared a bit more, and now he could see a woman's face covered in dusty smudges, studying him as she leaned closer. Judd wondered if he'd died and gone to cowboy heaven. Surely this couldn't be real.

'You're a bloody mess,' the apparition spoke again. 'I guess I'll have to try and get you back to my place . . . or maybe get a shovel and bury you, if you don't make it. You think you can stand up if I help you?'

'I'm . . . not sure.' Judd groaned.

'Come on, try. Sit up first, then we'll go from there.'

He rolled over and got on his knees, fighting to rise, while the woman hooked her arms under his, straining to lift him. 'Come on, cowboy! All the way up!'

Finally Judd stood shakily upright, as she propped him up and walked him to his horse. Grabbing him by the seat of his pants, she grunted, pushing him higher, and finally into the saddle; then she took his horse's reins and climbed on her own horse, and led them away from the cedar grove, where he would surely have died.

Judd was still barely conscious half an hour later, when she reined the horses to a stop. He tried focusing his eyes on the low log dugout with a dirt roof, almost invisible down the deep ravine. While helping him down, he did notice for the first time that she wore a low-slung leather gun belt with a pistol sticking up out of the holster.

'Lean down, and I'll get you inside,' she said, pulling his arm over her shoulder, slowly walking through the door, lowering him on to a bed against one wall. 'I've got to do something about this bleeding. Much more if it and you won't be having to worry about whether tomorrow will ever come, or not.'

Those were the last words Judd heard before the room went dark and he lost consciousness again.

The following evening, he awoke to the smell of something delicious cooking. He stared at the low log roof over his head, slowly becoming aware that the woman was standing on the far side of the room with her back to him, busy stirring a pot on a small wood stove. The small single lamp hanging from the ceiling cast moving shadows across the room. He tried to speak, but only managed a croak from his dry mouth. She heard it and turned around.

'I'd say it's time you woke up. I did a little more doctoring on you while you were out. I think I've got the bleeding stopped. You pulled out half your stitches riding. You better just lie still and let that wound heal up. Do you have a name, cowboy?'

'It's . . . Judd Miller. How long . . . have I been out?'

'Most of two days. If that bullet wound had been just a couple of inches deeper into your body, you'd be dead by now. Even as it is, gangrene could set in. I'll have to keep an eye on it and clean it every day.'

As Judd became more conscious, questions began flooding in. He had so many, he didn't know where to start. 'You know my name . . . what's yours?'

She crossed the room with a steaming bowl of soup in her hands. 'It's Lacey Dale, or at least it was, before I was married.'

'You're married?'

'I said "was". I'm not now. My husband, Jim Langley, was a shotgun guard for the Gamble and Gates stage line, but he was killed in a hold-up two years ago. The company said they thought the gang that held up the stage might be led by a man named Cayce Sloat, but there's no law anywhere around here to do anything about it.'

Judd pulled himself up higher, stiffening at the sound of that name. 'You sure of that name?'

'That's what they told me.' She shrugged slightly, handing him the bowl and spoon.

'Sloat's dead.'

She stared back at Judd, eyes suddenly wide in disbelief. 'How could you know anything about that?'

'Because I killed him.'

'You what!'

'Sloat and I shot it out up in Hang Town. That's how I caught this bullet. He just wasn't fast enough to do it twice. I was.'

Lacey retreated back across the room to the table. Sitting in a chair, her eyes were still locked on Miller. 'You're telling me you killed the man who killed my husband, and now I find you and I'm trying to save you? That's unbelievable, and if you're telling me the truth, something like this doesn't happen by chance. It's too incredible to believe. It has to be meant to

70

happen this way.'

'I don't know about that, but Sloat is dead and buried by now. I'm certain about that.'

Lacey couldn't believe the sudden turn of events. She lowered her head in both hands, shaking it back and forth, as her mind ran wild. Out of the few people scattered across this vast and lonely land, she'd found this wounded cowboy and taken him in. She was no fool, and didn't believe in black magic, but this eerie turn of events had to mean something else unforeseen was going to happen too. She wondered what that could possibly be.

Since her husband's murder, the once startlingly attractive woman had been forced to survive on her own, making a living any way she could. Her frilly dresses were cut up and used for other purposes. She was reduced to wearing a man's flannel shirt, pants and pull-on boots. Her long auburn hair, once combed and washed frequently, had grown out, and barely fitted under her beat-up cowboy hat. The transformation was so sudden and complete, that the few people who knew her hardly recognized her any more. Jim Langley had just begun to build the dugout cabin when he was killed. His plan was to make it much larger and more comfortable. When Lacey moved in on her own, she picked up a shovel, hammer and nails, and went to work, trying to salvage the dream they'd had together. At the age of twenty-nine, circumstances had forced Lacey Dale to become a reluctant tom boy.

*

Over the next three weeks Judd steadily regained his health and his wound began to heal. The odd couple thrown together by fate, destiny, or whatever it was, made no plans of any kind about what might happen next. Each seemed content not to speculate out loud as to whether he would finally saddle up and ride away, or stay for other reasons. Both lived from one day to the next, slowly gaining trust in each other to the point where Judd told her about the death of his brother, and how he'd ended up having the show-down with Cayce Sloat.

'My God, we've both been touched by the death of people we've loved, through no fault of our own.' She shook her head, while they sat at a small table after a dinner of sage hen stew. 'There's nothing I can do about what happened to my husband, but there is for you. You can go back and try to right the wrongs, and maybe even reclaim your property. If that's what you mean to do, I'd like to do it with you. There's nothing much left for me here, except this old dugout. My hopes died with Jim.'

Judd studied her for a moment before answering. 'You want to invite yourself to go back with me to the killing that's likely to take place? Because that's the way it's going to be. You'd better think twice about what you're asking for, Lacey.'

'I've seen death close up. I know the pain and loss, but I'm still here, managing to keep my head up, even if I do have to dress like a man and sometimes act like one, too. I'm not going to give up on life just because I'm a woman.'

72

Miller didn't answer for a moment. When he did, it was short and to the point.

'No, I guess you're not.'

Lacey woke one morning to the sudden sound of rapid gunfire close outside the dugout. Fear instantly gripped her as she kicked the covers off, grabbing the shotgun kept next to the bed, calling out for Judd as she ran for the door. Bursting through the piece of heavy canvas that served as a door, she saw Judd standing forty feet away with a smoking six-gun in his hand.

'What in the world are you doing?' she demanded, as he reloaded the pistol.

'I wanted to see if I'd lost any speed after laying around for so long.'

She lowered her head in relief, slowly trying to calm herself down. 'Well, have you?'

'It feels pretty good. I had to find out for myself. These days, just about everything I do seems to end up with me holding a six-gun in my hand. I don't expect that to change any time soon, so I had to get back to it. Sorry if I startled you. Is there any kind of town anyplace around here?'

'There is, if you want to call it that. Alkali used to be a stage stop, when they came through here. After several hold-ups and the death of my husband, they shut it down. Before that, years ago, I'm told they had mule teams hauling borax out of there. That ended, too. All that's left now is a Mexican cantina, a couple of dry goods stores, a sometimes blacksmith's shop and horse stable, plus some empty buildings that used to be stores. It isn't much to look at, that's for sure.'

'I need another shirt. This one's a mess, with all the dried blood. Even you washing it didn't take the stain out. How far away is it?'

'A day's ride.'

'How about we leave in the morning. They don't have any law there, do they?'

'No, what for? Nothing ever happens, and there's no one who's going to pay for it either. Could I ask you something personal?' She surprised him with the question.

'I imagine you can. You've been taking care of me long enough. I at least owe you that much.'

'Did I just find a wounded cowboy, or are you a real gun fighter, Judd?'

He took in a slow breath. The question was so sudden, it took him by surprise. The long, silent stare as they faced each other only grew more uncomfortable.

'Understand this, Lacey. I didn't ask for any of what's happened to me. I was a cowboy rancher along with my brother, like I said. Sooner or later I'm going back to Red Bluffs, to find out who killed my brother, and why. If I have to keep using this six-gun to do that and remain free, I will. I'm not going to let some back-shooter put me six feet under because I wasn't fast enough to stop him. For now, tomorrow let's take that ride into Alkali.'

CHAPTER SIX

The late afternoon sun dimmed behind a dirty sky driven by swirling winds. Through the veil of dust, Lacey and Judd saw the first low silhouette of buildings ahead, and a little later rode into Alkali. Its single dirt street was empty except for three hard-ridden horses standing head down at a hitching rail in front of an adobe building with a faded sign 'Manzanita Cantina' painted over the entrance. At the far end of the street Judd noticed a boarded-up church with its steeple leaning dangerously, ready to fall. Clearly God-fearing people had already given up on the small town, leaving it to the designs of men.

'Where's the dry goods store?' Judd asked.

'Right across the street,' she pointed, as they reined to a halt and dismounted. Climbing the steps up on to the boardwalk, they stepped inside Mort Beckman's dry goods store.

The old man looked up at the ringing of the little bell over the door. He appeared as old and bent over as the store itself. He used a cane to get around even inside the store. What few shirts he had were kept on a shelf, behind a hand-cranked cash register. Judd asked to see what he had, and tried on three before he found one that fitted.

'Say, that's a real nasty wound you got there mister,' the proprietor nodded, as Judd buttoned up the new shirt.

'It could have been worse,' Judd answered in a matter of fact way.

'I ain't seen you for a good while, Miss Dale. How you been?' Beckman turned to Lacey.

'I'm all right,' she smiled back.

'You still livin' way out there in that dugout?'

'For now, I am. But maybe not much longer. This might be the last time I ever see Alkali again.'

'Well, the few people left around here sure would miss your pretty face, if you did go. I remember those pretty dresses you always wore, before your husband was killed.'

'That was a different time, and so was Alkali, back then.'

'It sure was. I'm even thinkin' about closing down this old store myself. Soon the whole darn town will dry up and blow away, just like everything else around here. If I don't see you again, here's hoping the world treats you better than this town did. Your husband was a real good man. A lot of the goodness in Alkali died when he was shot down.'

'Thank you for saying so, Mr Beckman. Jim had many friends here.'

'I mean it. I'm not just saying that. Those good ol'

days are gone, and this town is worse off for it. It's dying out a little at a time, just like the people still left around here.'

Judd paid for the shirt, and Lacey said her good-byes to the old man before they started for the door. They were making their way out of Beckman's just as three young Mexican *vaqueros* stepped outside the Manzanita across the street, joking and talking loudly at each other, until they saw Lacey across the street by the horses. With a bellyful of potent mescal, the trio eyed her salaciously, before one of them shouted out, smiling broadly.

'Hey gringo, why do you dress your *señorita* in a man's baggy pants, shirt and boots. Why are you trying to hide her like dat?'

Judd's face instantly flushed red with anger at the insult to Lacey. He turned away from saddling up, and faced the three men. Lacey instantly saw the look on his face, reaching to grab him by the shoulder.

'Don't listen to them. They're drunk. Come on, let's saddle up and get out of here, Judd.'

'You better listen to the *señorita*, gringo. You don't want my *amigo* here, Juanito, to have to teach you a lesson, do you? He is very fast with a pistola.' A second Mexican spoke up, putting his arm on Juanito Cisnero's shoulder, smiling back through broad white teeth.

Judd had been pushed far enough. He took a few more steps farther out into the street, as Lacey tried calling him back. 'Stay back out of the way,' he ordered. 'Get behind the horses.'

77

As she did so, he called out an answer. 'You three jaybirds are a little too far north of the border. You'd better get back to whatever mud hut you call home. This isn't Mexico. I'd say it's time you learned that.'

The smile on the faces of the trio suddenly disappeared. Cisneros whispered something to his pals about teaching this insulting Americano a lesson, right here on the dirt street of town, adding that he wouldn't need any help doing so. He adjusted his gun belt before stepping off into the street, the smile returning to his face.

'So, gringo, I just shoot you down in pieces, so you suffer more. And the *señorita* won't want to stay with a cripple. She is too young and beautiful to waste. Maybe I will take her back to Mexico with me, huh?'

'You make one move for that pistol, and you won't be riding anywhere. You and your friends better climb back on your horses and get out of here. Either that or your pals will have to buy a two-dollar blanket to bury you in.'

'OK, gringo. Now I will kill you for your disrespect. Are you ready to die?'

'I was born ready. Remember, you and your friends wanted it this way.'

The lean Mexican stood poised, legs slightly apart, ready to pull, his dark eyes riveted on the cowboy thirty feet away. Judd Miller would make the fourth man he'd killed, but he'd be the most enjoyable one of all. Cisneros was fast, real fast, and he knew it. His hand stabbed for the pistol, and he did get it clear of the holster, starting it up to fire, but the flash and

78

roar of Miller's six-gun beat him to it. The sudden smash of hot lead driving deep into his chest, drove him back, fighting to stay on his feet, as his pistol dropped to the ground and he followed it down, rolling on the dirt street.

Suddenly the scene turned into complete chaos. Lacey screamed as the Mexican's two *amigos* ran for cover left and right, pulling their pistols to fire. Judd dodged left, crouching slightly, firing a second and third shot, driving one of the men head first off the boardwalk down into the street, grabbing his stomach, screaming in pain. The third man was still running, frantically firing back, when the roar of a rifle shot from behind Judd's back shattered a glass window as the Mexican ran by, instantly convincing him to throw up his hands and drop his pistol, screaming in fear, suddenly facing two guns instead of one.

'Don't shoot . . . I'm disarmed!'

Judd turned just long enough to see Lacey holding the rifle to her shoulder, which she'd yanked from the scabbard on his horse. 'Keep him covered!' he shouted, walking across the street to where Cisneros lay shivering in death.

'I need . . . *medico* . . .' the dying man whispered, but the neat, .45-calibre hole in his fancy vest said different, and seconds later his eyes went blank in death.

Lacey prodded the last *vaquero* up to Judd, keeping the rifle barrel pressed hard on his back. His pleading eyes were wide with fear that he would be killed, too.

'Here's his pistol,' she handed Judd the Mexican's revolver. Holstering his own six-gun, Judd ejected all the bullets out of the Mexican's weapon and tossed it into a watering trough nearby.

'Please *señor*, do not kill me,' the *vaquero* pleaded. 'In the name of Santa Maria, I beg for mercy!'

Miller gave the terrified man a long, withering look. Seconds earlier this man would have shot down Judd and Lacey without a thought. Now he was pitifully begging for his life. Judd glanced at Lacey, then back to the man. 'You get on your horse, and get out of here before I change my mind. Don't look back. Just keep on riding, you understand?'

'*Sí señor. Muchas graçias.* I do it now, as you say.'

The *vaquero* quickly mounted his horse and whipped it away down the street in a rising cloud of dust. Miller turned back to Lacey, just as several store owners cautiously stepped out on to the boardwalk, now that all the killing was over.

'Let's get out of here, too. I have to say thanks, Lacey. I didn't expect you to pull that rifle out and start shooting. But I'm glad you did.'

She stared back at him without blinking, before speaking. 'I've already lost one man in my life who meant something to me. I didn't want to have that happen again.'

Her bold admission left Judd standing speechless. All he could do was nod slightly, and take her by the arm, heading for the horses to mount up. Starting down the street, one of the store owners called out to him. 'What are we supposed to do with those bodies?'

'Bury them,' Judd called back. 'It will give the good citizens of Alkali something to do besides watching the rest of this town die with them.'

Arriving back at the dugout, Judd was anxious to pack up and leave, fearing that the shootout in town might draw attention to him from a lot further away than just Alkali. That was a chance he could not take.

'I'd like to get out of here as soon as we can,' he told Lacey. 'There's nothing left around here for me, and I think we'd make a good pair. I saw that back in town, when I didn't expect it.'

'If that's what you mean to do, I want to go with you.'

'You know what you're letting yourself in for, don't you? When the day comes that I make it back to Red Bluffs, I'm a Wanted man, to be shot on sight. I want to make that plain right now. That's the kind of life you'd be letting yourself in for.'

'What kind of life do I have staying here? I'll take my chances with you, Judd. I understand the risks. It doesn't mean it has to turn out that way, does it?'

'Maybe not, but it will be hell, one way or the other.'

The pair stayed on at the dugout for the next two days, packing up what little goods and food they wanted to take with them. On the morning of the third day, they saddled up and left, giving the rough-hewn structure one last look as they rode away.

'Where are we going?' Lacey asked.

'I have a friend over the mountains, but we'll have to skirt the high country to get there, to avoid going through Hang Town, and that will make it a longer ride.'

'I thought you were a man without friends?' she kidded him with a small smile.

'I am, for the most part. I ran into this one by accident. He's a little on the unusual side, but I think you'll like him. I know he'll like you.'

'What's his name?'

'He calls himself Moses Canaan, but that's not his real name. It's one he gave to himself.'

'Is he a man with a fast gun, like you?'

Judd laughed out loud. 'Moses? No, his weapon is the bible, at least most of the time, if he doesn't fall back into his old ways. He's sort of a preacher of his own design. He put me up for a while when I needed it most.'

'Just like I did?'

'Yes, just like you did. Wait until you see where he lives.'

'Is it in a town?'

'Not exactly – he lives in a cave in the middle of the desert.'

'A cave!'

'That's what I said, but it's not what you think. It's really quite a place.'

It took Judd and Lacey three weeks of hard riding through bitter, thorny dry lowlands to skirt the mountains before Judd arrived back in country familiar to him, and headed for Moses' rock-bound home. The tall man in the stove-pipe hat saw distant dust plumes of riders coming closer. His eyes narrowed, and he shaded them with one hand, trying to make out who it was coming in. He recognized Judd's horse first, then the rider in the saddle, and his eyes widened as a big smile broke out on his face. Judd Miller was still alive, and he was even bringing in a friend to visit. When Judd had left, Moses had prayed that the Good Lord would protect him, and now his prayers had been answered. Moses did wonder who it was that the man who always rode alone, had riding with him. When the pair reined to a halt, he stepped forward, still smiling, reaching up with his hand and locking it in Judd's.

'You don't know how glad I am to see you again. When you left I wondered if you'd be all right. I see our saviour has done a splendid job looking over you.'

'How are you, Moses? It's good to see you again, too. I've brought someone with me,' he indicated over his shoulder.

Moses could not see Lacey's face because Judd's horse blocked his view. He stepped around the front of the animal, and then looked up, extending his hand. Suddenly his face registered surprise: this visitor might look like a man with that flannel shirt, boots and big cowboy hat shading her face, but all those curls sticking out from under the hat and that pretty face, said she was all woman. Moses quickly regained the power of speech.

83

'Well, I'll be dam. . . .' he caught himself, turning back to Miller. 'You never fail to surprise me, and you sure did it again this time. Both of you get down out of those saddles, and come inside, after we take care of your horses.'

Once inside the spacious cave, Lacey took it all in, wide eyed in surprise, as Moses showed her round, and how everything he'd put together worked. He might be a man striving to live by God's command-ments, but he could not ignore Lacey's rough-hewn beauty, as he led her around. Eventually he had to ask her the question that had been haunting him since they first met.

'May I ask you something personal?' he hoped she wouldn't be offended.

'Yes, what it is?'

'Is there some reason you hide how pretty you are by dressing up like a man?'

She smiled at the odd compliment. 'It's because when my husband was killed, all I had left was our half-finished dugout, and most of his clothes. We had both worked on it, and I wore his clothes because I was getting dirty and sweaty each day. I couldn't get much done in a frilly dress and lace-up shoes! Then when I was alone, I had to do what I could, working at anything I could in a man's world, and it was just easier to wear what I've got on.'

'Thank you for telling me that, and I'm sorry to hear about such a tragedy. But I have to say I still think it's a shame you cover yourself up. You're too pretty for that. Please don't take offence at my saying so. May I call you Miss Lacey?'

'Of course you can, and thank you for being so nice about it.'

That evening while eating dinner around a crackling fire at the front of the cave, Moses asked Judd about what happened after he rode out of Dry Wells. Miller looked back at his friend over the dancing flames, wondering if he should tell him the whole story, including what had happened up in Hang Town, and even Alkali, too. Lacey stopped eating and stared at Judd, waiting to see how much he would reveal. He put down his plate, deciding not to hide any of it. He began explaining about the shoot-out up in Hang Town with Cayce Sloat, and the Mexicans in Alkali.

Moses sat listening without saying a word until he had finished. The tall man took in a long, slow breath, attempting to put words together that might make some sense, while trying to avoid being too critical of his friend. He rubbed his hands together, beginning: 'It seems that fate has decided to make you someone who might spend the rest of his life living with a six-gun in his hand, but I know you better than that. I also know that fate doesn't always have to win, either. A man can change things in his life, and live differently. I know the hand you were dealt, with your brother's murder and your goal to set things right and make someone pay for that. But I have to tell you that I believe the day will come when you hang up that hog-leg for good, and live like you were meant to.'

Judd took a sip from his coffee cup, understanding that Moses' words were only expressing concern about his well-being. Putting down the cup, he stared back at his lanky friend. 'I didn't ask to live this way. Other people played those cards you were just talking about. But I'm not going to stop until I get my ranch back, and until the men who started this are either in jail, or dead. I'm going back to Red Bluffs, and coming here was only the start of that journey. Nothing is going to stop me now, even if I die trying.'

'Yes, I know that, Judd. But you can't just shoot your way back into town. From what you've already told me, your name is likely being spread on every wanted poster between here and Mexico, whether you know it or not. Sooner or later some posse is going to catch up to you, and you've got to find some other way to right the wrongs that were done to you and your brother, without using a flaming six-gun.'

'If there is another way, I don't know what it is. When I get back to Red Bluffs, maybe I can find one, but I doubt it. Men there used their kind of law against me. I'm going to use mine back in the same way.'

Moses leaned away from the heat of the fire, closing his eyes, trying to think of some way to help this man he'd grown so fond of. For a long time no one spoke. Only the sound of snapping flames disturbed the quiet chill of night. When he opened them again, he looked back at Judd, with his solution.

86

'It's been said that a man must travel through hell before he can get to heaven. I imagine they must have had a man like you in mind, when that was first said. It may take your six-gun and my bible, but the only way all this can see a fitting end, is if I go back with you, to help out. After you get rested up for a few days, all three of us will leave together for Red Bluffs!'

Judd spent the next two days trying to talk Moses out of his promise to ride with him and Lacey, but try as he might, Moses refused to budge. He'd made up his mind to try and save his friend whatever might lay ahead, and he meant to see it through to the end.

The horses had a good feed and were well rested, the morning of the trio's departure. Moses had loaded his wagon with enough provisions and water to take on the same perilous desert journey that had almost taken Judd's life on his first crossing. Then as Judd walked around the back of the wagon, he saw the tall preacher loading a shotgun wrapped in a blanket into the back, under several food bags.

'What are you going to do with that?' Miller asked.

Moses, caught by surprise, turned to face him with an odd look on his face as he searched for a quick answer. 'Well . . . I might shoot us . . . a sage hen for dinner, if I get the chance.'

'Sage hen, huh?'

'Yes. If I get the chance.'

'I hope that's the only thing you'll use it on. I'd hate to think you might do something else with it.'

'So would I, Judd. You know I'm a man of peace.'

87

'Yes, I do. I hope you keep it that way.'

'Can I ask how long it took you to cross the desert, when we first met up?'

'I believe it was a little over a week and a half. I was stretched pretty thin when we first met up, so I'm not certain.'

'I see.' He hesitated, pulling at his chin. 'I believe we should be able to do it in about the same time, or maybe even a little bit better. You two saddle up and let's get to it.'

Once mounted, Moses snapped the reins down on his big mule, as the wagon creaked forward, with the riders in the lead. They hadn't gone far when Moses began loudly singing 'Onward Christian Soldiers'. Lacey looked over at Judd with a small smile on her face. He glanced back with a small shrug. How could he complain when he had God riding with them?

Each day as the wagon and riders moved farther out into the vast sandy plains, Judd's memory of his struggle to outrun the posse led by Jared Bass returned, and the hardships he'd faced trying to outlast the men riding behind trying to catch up. With Moses' wagon filled with provisions and water, this crossing was a far different event, despite those bitter thoughts. At night when they made camp under a velvet black sky blazing with diamond bright stars, Moses did the cooking, and they washed down the welcome provender with cool water from the big, canvas-wrapped casket on the side of the wagon.

During meals they discussed how Judd wanted to

return to Red Bluffs without being seen, to learn the reason for Randall's death, and for the night-time attack on their ranch, an attack that nearly took his life, too. It was decided the three of them would camp well out of town, letting Moses and Lacey take the wagon each day into town because they were not known by anyone. Moses suggested he could do some preaching from the tailgate on the back of his wagon, to become a regular fixture around town, making it easier to ask questions without becoming suspicious to anyone. Lacey would pretend to do some shopping for the same reason, while Judd stayed out of sight.

On the ninth day of their journey, the endless monotony of flat, desert tan was finally interrupted by the distant silhouette of purple mountains rising ahead signalling they were nearly across. Not far into those mountains lay the watered heights of Red Bluffs, unsuspecting of its new arrivals. Starting up into the first foothills three days later, desert heat faded into chilling night-time temperatures that demanded a crackling evening fire to keep warm. As they ate dinner, Moses questioned his cowboy friend.

'How far away from town would you say we are now?'

'Another two days.'

'When we get there, where do you want to set up camp outside of town?' Lacey wondered.

'There's a timber ridge above our ranch, or what's left of it. We can camp there without being seen, while I keep an eye on my property, in case anyone is doing something with it. Someone wanted my brother and me off that land bad enough to kill for it. That's something maybe you and Moses might get some word about when you're in town. I might try coming into town at night, and keep out of sight. There are still some things and places I want to go to, without being seen. Randall and I had friends there. Maybe someone can help me while keeping it quiet.'

CHAPTER SEVEN

Two days after their arrival at Red Bluffs, Sunday midday found Moses standing on the tailgate of his slogan-painted wagon on main street, preaching to a curious crowd of onlookers. As he harangued the sinners of their certain fate if they didn't change their ways, more people gathered around to hear his stirring words of redemption. One of the new arrivals was especially sceptical of the tall man in his frock coat. Cyrus Toomey eyed Moses suspiciously, wondering if he was just half crazy, or actually lived by the tenets of the Good Book that he kept threatening the crowd with.

'Hey, Mayor,' one man called out. 'What do you think about all this?' He pointed to Moses, who also heard the call, remembering what Judd had said about him.

'And you, Mr Mayor,' Moses immediately turned on Toomey. 'Can you say you've lived an exemplary life free of sin, while helping your fellow men?'

Toomey glared back at being singled out, while

those around him turned to hear his answer.

'Can you speak, sir?' Moses kept at him. 'Surely a man entrusted to be mayor has to be a man right with God, or he'd be a charlatan and a Judas to his own people. Wouldn't you agree to that, sir?'

Toomey's face reddened in anger. His nostrils flared while his mouth twisted in sudden hate, at being called out and embarrassed by this uninvited troublemaker.

'You're all talk and hot air,' Cyrus yelled back, shaking a raised fist at the preacher. 'I'll bet you're the biggest sinner in this whole town!'

'Yes, I have sinned. But I've regretted it, and made myself right with the Lord. Can you say here and now you've done the same? I'm sure all these folks standing here would like to hear you say so. I know I would.'

'I don't give a damn what you'd like to hear. If you're smart, you'll fold up your wagon and get out of town, before I have you arrested!'

'Arrested for what? Asking a simple question of the town's leading citizen? You'd have to arrest this whole town, if that's the case.' Moses chuckled at his own quick retort.

Bested to the point of frustration, Toomey flung a fist at Moses, before pushing his way out of the growing throng of people. Half a block down the street he ran into Jared Bass. Pulling him quickly aside, he blurted out a quick order.

'See that religious quack down the block?' he jerked his head toward the crowd. 'Get rid of him.'

'How?'

'Any way you can. Just remove him, and fast. I don't want to see or hear of him around here again, you understand?'

'Yes, I do.'

'All right, get to it.'

Bass walked down the street to where Moses was still preaching his non-stop, religious gift of the gab. He eyed the tall man and his painted wagon. One look was all he needed to know that Toomey's order would be a quick and easy one to carry out.

Moses spent the rest of that Sunday moving around town, observing everything he could while talking to people to see if he could learn anything about what happened to the Miller brothers and their property outside town. Most people avoided giving answers, although everyone knew about Randall's killing, and the gun battle Judd had before he got away. Sundown came fast after his busy day. He was anxious to get back to Judd and Lacey, and in particular to tell them about his verbal exchange with Toomey. He flapped the reins down on the big mule's back, and the wagon rattled down the street, heading out of town, as the first long shadows of evening slowly engulfed the town buildings.

A darkening sky began to light up with the first blink of stars, followed by a chilly evening wind with it. Moses pulled up his collar against it. Half an hour later rounding a bend in the road, he saw the shadowy figure of three men on horseback blocking his advance. Pulling back on the reins, he called out to let him pass. They did not move as he came to a stop in front of them.

'Hey, preacher,' one man called back, 'here's a little message from the mayor. Get out of town and stay out, if you know what's good for you!'

Before Moses could answer, the sudden swish of a lariat came whirling out of the dark, encircling him, pulled instantly tight, as the rider spurred his horse away, yanking Moses from the wagon seat. Flying through the air, he crashed to the ground, and was then dragged at a gallop over rocks and ruts, beating him bloody as he twisted and turned out of control.

After a long run down the road, Bass yanked his horse around, dragging Moses back until his clothes were torn to bloody rags, and he lost consciousness for several moments. When he partially regained his senses through a wall of growing pain, he heard one of the horsemen above him speak.

'This is your last warning, preacher. We see you in town or anyplace else again, and we'll bury you in that wagon of yours!'

Moses lay on his back, staring up into the night, barely able to move. But he was conscious enough to hear one of the men joke as they kicked their horses away. 'Nice work, Jared. That ought to put the fear of God into him!' Their laughter faded away along with the hoof beats.

The tall man tried to pull himself up, but every time he did, sudden knives of pain cut through him to the bone, until he could barely breathe, and he fell back down. He knew he had to get back to camp and help, or he would die where he lay. Summoning every ounce of strength he had, he took in a faltering breath and began praying out loud.

'Help me . . . Lord. Help me . . . rise.'

Again he tried to sit up so he could roll over on to his hands and knees and crawl to the wagon, but he collapsed half way up. Desperate for an answer, his mind struggled for another way. Then suddenly, hearing his mule moving nervously in its traces, he thought of a possible solution: if he couldn't make it to the wagon, maybe he could get the wagon to come to him!

He took in another stabbing breath before calling out: 'J-a-a-k-e . . . come here . . . boy. J-a-a-k-e . . . come on . . . you can . . . do it.'

The rattling sound of the wagon moving forwards gave Moses a burst of new hope, until moments later the dark shadow of the mule and wagon loomed over him, coming to a stop.

'Stay still . . . now . . . don't move.'

Moses reached up, grabbing one of the thick wooden spokes on the wheel, pulling himself higher inch by excruciating inch, until his hand clutched the metal seat rail. He had to make it into that seat, or die trying.

Judd and Lacey stood around the small fire warming their hands, hidden from view below in the valley. 'Shouldn't Moses be back by now?' Lacey wondered out loud, the worry in her voice obvious.

'If he doesn't show up soon, I'll have to saddle up

and go look for him.' Judd answered, just as he heard the first sound of the wagon coming closer. Stepping away from the fire, he called out to Moses without getting an answer.

'It's about time you . . .' Judd stopped, seeing the preacher slumped over on the wagon seat, face down. He ran for the wagon pulling himself up in the seat, lifting Moses in his arms. 'What happened, Moses? Can you speak?'

Carefully lifting Moses' limp body down from the wagon, Judd lowered him on to a blanket spread next to the fire, where he could take his first good look at his friend's bloody face and torn clothes. A sudden cry came from Lacey's lips as she kneeled closer, putting her hand to her mouth.

'Get me some water and a cloth,' Judd ordered. 'I'll try to clean him up and see how bad he is. Looks like he's torn up from head to toe.'

Moses moaned, barely aware of where he was, while Judd and Lacey worked over him. 'My God, what could have happened to him?' Lacey slowly cleaned the blood off the tall man's bloody face.

'He's been rope dragged behind a horse. That's the only way his clothes and the rest of him could end up looking like this,' Judd shook his head.

'But who could even think of doing something like this, and why?'

'I don't know, but he was in town most of the day. He must have rubbed someone the wrong way, or asked a question no one wanted to answer.'

Moses groaned, his eyes opening only to slits in his

swollen face. He coughed up blood, struggling to spit out just one word, as his hand came up and gripped Judd by his jacket, trying to pull him closer. 'Jar . . . ed' he finally managed to blurt out, before collapsing back down on the blanket.

'You mean Jared Bass?' Judd quickly questioned. 'Is that who did this to you?'

Moses nodded, closing his eyes again, as Judd looked over at Lacey, before slowly getting to his feet, a grim look of determination coming over his face. Lacey had seen that look before, back in Alkali, moments before the gunfight with the three Mexicans. She stood with him, trying to stop what she knew was coming.

'Don't go, Judd. Don't take the chance something could happen to you, too. Stay here with me and help me work on Moses. Please, listen to me!'

'I'm going. You take care of him until I get back. I won't be gone too long.'

'If something happens to you, Moses and I would be done for. We'd have to pack up and leave. Nothing would ever get done about your property, and what happened to your brother. Is it really worth risking all that?'

'I've got to go. I don't expect you to understand why. I can't let this pass like it never happened. Jared Bass is the man who tried to kill me, and may have had a hand in killing my brother. He's going to pay for it. It's a debt long overdue. I'll be back, I promise I will.'

Lacey's shoulders sagged and her head fell to her

chest. She took in a long, deep breath, trying to think of something else to say. She couldn't. Instead she watched in silence as Miller saddled up his horse and rode away into the night, without saying another word. Turning back to the fire she fed it new wood, the rising flames lighting fresh tears running down her checks as she went back to work on Moses.

Judd reached town, riding down deserted back streets one block over from the row of lamp-lit whiskey houses and gambling dens on Main Street. Stopping at one alley, he tied his horse to the hitch rail and entered the passageway between the buildings, walking to its end where it reached the still busy front street. Across from here he could see the Silver Slipper saloon, busy with boisterous customers coming and going in and out the front door. To his left on his side of the street, just one door down, the Slipper's main competitor, the Rough and Ready Bar, also hosted its share of night-time gamblers and drinkers. He well remembered that the Rough and Ready was one of Jared Bass's main watering holes.

Pulling his hat down low over his face and his jacket collar higher, Miller stepped out on to the boardwalk, walking the few steps to the front window of the busy saloon, peering into the big room's smoky interior. His eyes searched the room through the dirty window, until coming to the bar where George La Mont, owner of the establishment, was busy moving back and forth behind the oak countertop, pouring drinks and collecting money for the big cash register against the mirrored wall at his back.

Judd pushed his face closer to the glass, studying the outline of one big man at the far end of the bar with his back to him. He stood head and shoulders above other men, and the tan steamer on his head said it could only be Jared Bass. Miller's jaw tightened, watching men gathered around Bass, laughing and slapping him on the back as he retold the tale of how he'd run that phony preacher out of town.

Judd knew he had to get Bass out of the bar alone without anyone else seeing him. As he tried to come up with a way to do it, a young teenage boy out on the town for the first time to see the sights, came walking down the street towards him. The kid was stopping and gawking into each brightly lit storefront window, and by the time he'd reached the Rough and Ready, Miller had the plan he needed.

'Hey, kid,' Judd waved him closer.

'Yeah, what is it, mister?'

Judd dug into his pants pocket and came up with a few coins. 'Here's six bits. I want you to go in here and tell that tall man at the bar that an old friend is waiting outside for him. You think you can do that?'

'Sure I can, for six bits.' The young man eagerly took the money, shoving it into his pocket, before heading for the front door.

Judd quickly walked back into the dark alley, edging up just close enough to see around the corner on to the boardwalk. Two minutes later, Bass walked out with the young man at his side, both looking up and down the street. Bass said something to the kid who shrugged, then started back up the street alone. As the big man turned to go back inside, Judd called out. 'Hey Bass, over here!'

Jared turned on his boot heel, looking towards the narrow passageway. 'Who is it?' He started towards the alley, coming closer, when a hand suddenly reached out and grabbed him by his jacket collar – Judd yanked him to the side and swung his heavy six-gun down across his face, knocking him unconscious so he fell in a heap. Judd pulled him into the alley out of sight, then ran back down the alley to his horse, which he led back to Bass's prone form. He quickly tied Bass's hands and feet, then untied his bandana and stuffed it in his mouth. Taking his lariat off the horse, Judd looped one end tightly round the big man's feet, then quickly mounting up, made two turns around the saddle horn with the other end, pulling it tight. Spurring the horse forwards, he dragged Bass's body out into the middle of the street, then kicked the animal into a hoof-pounding gallop.

Bass's body twisted and turned, taking the same kind of beating he'd given Moses earlier that evening. At the far end of town, Judd yanked the horse around, spurring it back down the three block-long main street on a second fast run, Jared's body twisting and crashing down again and again until Judd pulled to a stop back in front of the Rough and Ready. One quick rope loop loosened the lariat from the unconscious man's feet. Miller quickly coiled it up and spurred his horse away again, out of town, into the night.

Customers ran out of the saloon into the street

and surrounded the broken, bloody body of Jared Bass, still tied up hand and foot, moaning in misery. 'Who in hell was that rider?' one called out.

'I don't know for sure,' another man answered. 'But what little look I got at him almost makes me swear it was Judd Miller!'

'Judd Miller? Naw, he's probably dead by now, just like his brother. It couldn't have been him.'

The sun had barely lit the rooftops in Red Bluffs the following morning, as Cyrus Toomey stood staring down at Jared Bass, heavily bandaged and lying in his bed in the small house he rented at the end of town.

'What do you mean, you don't know who did this to you? Are you blind?' Toomey's mocking voice made his displeasure and concern obvious.

'I was bushwhacked from out of the dark, I'm tellin' you. Someone hit me with an ax handle, or something. Look at my face. The rest of me ain't much better, either!'

Toomey leaned down closer, emphasizing his words. 'There is no one in town with enough guts to do this to you. What about that scarecrow preacher, could he have had a hand in it?'

'Hell, no. When I got done dragging him, he couldn't even get to his feet. We left him lying in the road. For all I know, he might still be out there.'

Toomey began pacing the room, talking to himself. 'None of this makes any sense. I've got to get to the bottom of it, and fast. My contact with the Western Cascade railroad people could be coming even sooner than I thought and I can't have anything getting in the way of it now. How long before you can get back on your feet again?'

'Not this week. I'm lucky I didn't get my neck broke. Doc Owens says I have to stay like this for at least one more week. I can't even move without feeling like I'm busted up from top to bottom. I have to use a bedpan because I can't stand up. Looks like you're on your own until then.'

In the hidden camp outside town, Moses, too, was suffering from being horse dragged, lying in his bed in his wagon. As Lacey spoon fed him hot broth, Judd stood listening to every word the preacher could get out.

'I talked to a lot of people . . . in town yesterday, before I was jumped last night. Two businessmen mentioned something to me that might be . . . important, especially to you, Judd.'

'If you're up to it, tell me about it.'

'They said they'd heard the railroad might be coming . . . this way. You know what that could mean about . . . any property they might want to . . . buy up, don't you?'

The stunning news instantly got Judd's attention. He pulled up a small stool, sitting on it close to the bed. 'That's something Toomey would likely know about,' he nodded, thinking out loud. 'If you're right about this, I've got to find out where they mean to lay steel.'

'They said . . . they thought the railhead was about

102

fifty miles east of here . . . somewhere down in the flatlands out of . . . the mountains.'

'Can you two make it all right, if I leave here?' Judd asked.

Lacey looked up with worry in her eyes, but not about Judd's possibly leaving for a while. 'If you do go, there's a chance someone might recognize you from a wanted poster. If that happened our very reason for making the trip here would be over, and you'd likely be facing jail, a trial, or worse. If something like that did take place, I'd never forgive myself for letting you go.'

'Nothing like that will happen. I won't let it, but I've got to find out if what Moses heard is true. It could answer a lot of questions, about what has happened to my brother and me.'

'You be . . . double careful,' Moses tries to rise, but sank back down, his face grimacing in pain. Instead he reached up, gripping Judd's jacket with a bony hand. 'Get back here safe, you hear? I'll pray for you every day . . . you're gone.'

'I will. You rest easy and let Lacey take care of you. I'll be careful.'

Miller left that same morning, riding fast and hard the next four days down out of the timbered heights of Red Bluffs, until rolling grasslands of an endless prairie spread before him, filling the horizon. He wasn't certain how far ahead he had to go, or even exactly in what direction tracks of steel were being laid. Each morning he took bearings from the rising sun in the east, riding on line of sight until it burned out behind him at sundown. Small bands of buffalo parted and ran as he passed, until mid-day on the eighth, when the dark green smudge of low trees ahead rose up out of the sea of grass, the first sign of civilization he'd seen.

Prairie Creek was hardly a town. A small general store by the name of 'Hall's Mercantile', a sometimes blacksmith shop, a horse corral, and three empty wooden buildings ready to fall down, met Judd's eyes when he rode in. Tying his horse at the hitching rail in front of the store, he stepped inside Hall's Mercantile. The musty odour of disuse matched the dusty interior.

Josiah Hall stood behind the counter, eyeing him as he started across the creaking floor.

'Howdy, stranger,' Hall forced a weak smile through wire-rimmed glasses, quickly noticing Miller's cross-draw gun rig. 'You sure ain't from around here, I can see that right now. What can I do for you?'

'I can use a good feed of oats for my horse, and something for myself, too. I'd also like some information, if you have any.'

'About what?' Hall raised his eyebrows.

'I've been told the railroad is pushing its way west from someplace out here. Do you know where that might be?'

'Well, I do know some of it. I'm told the railroad is north of here about fifteen or twenty miles. They passed that way two weeks ago. Felix Hays, who lives up there, was in here and told me that. He also said they're laying a mile of steel a day. If that's so, they'll be farther out by now. About the food, we don't have any restaurant, but I guess you can see that for yourself. I'm about all that's left here, and I don't know how much longer I might want to keep the door open, either. I got beans and corn and some salted beef out back. You can use sacked oats for your horse, if you like.'

Judd put the feed bag on his horse, before going back inside, buying supplies to put in his saddle-bags. After paying off Hall, he went back outside with the proprietor following him. 'You've got some tall riding to do catching up with them railroad people. Good luck, young feller!'

Miller gave him a quick wave, kicking his horse north out of town. Two days later Judd saw an elevated gravely berm rising out of tall grass ahead. When he reached it riding up on top, he looked down at shiny new steel rails curving away westward until they disappeared out of sight. He hesitated only long enough to take a quick pull on his water bag, before urging the horse down off the tracks, running parallel with the roadway, at a steady gallop.

Many miles away in his plushly appointed private railroad car, Farris Whitmore Thurston, president of the Western Cascade Railroad Company, lounged in a padded chair eating breakfast made by his private cook. As he ate he looked out of the window watching wagons, mules, and his gangs of men hauling steel rails with rail tongs, thick, wooden ties and heavy caskets of thumb thick spikes to spike the rails down with. Even in the confines of his private car, he could hear the bell-like ring of spike mauls driving spikes down on new steel not far ahead.

F.W., as his friends and business associates called him, was a 'hands on' man. An enterprise as costly and daring as this one, bringing a new railroad line across the vastness of the prairie, could not be left to chance or to the decisions of other men. His entire fortune was at stake. Instead, F.W. would run the show himself. Each day after breakfast he donned polished, hand-made, knee-high leather boots and his expensive suit, topped off by a wide-brimmed hat specially ordered to his size and tan colour, and took personal charge of the working gangs. He did this standing on a flatbed railcar where new rails were being laid, with a megaphone to his mouth calling out orders, and pointing with a golden-knobbed cane.

Some grumbling by gang foremen was inevitable. But Thurston got track laid, and on the schedule he'd set for himself. That was all that mattered as he aimed for that first vital notch in the beginning heights of the Rocky Mountains, somewhere ahead in the town named Red Bluffs. If he could drive into the mountains at that precise point, his maps showed that the climb over the top could be the success he needed so badly, and would beat his only competition, the six-horse stagecoach, by a week and one hundred miles.

CHAPTER EIGHT

The endless sweat and toil of the rail gangs, largely made up of Chinese labourers, had been so intense that they were running out of supplies and material, forcing F.W. to realize they would be spiking down the last few miles of steel rails ahead until the supply train caught up. To speed up that delivery, he rode two days by horseback back to the supply yard, immediately taking personal charge of loading the flatbed railcars. Once the goods were tied down, he rode the smoke-belching engine back west, staying up in the engine cab with the engineer and fireman, stoking the firebox. He loved the rumble and roar of the locomotive as it picked up speed, with the trailing flatbeds, loaded high, shaking and swaying behind them.

Judd saw the dissipating cloud of black smoke over a rise in the tracks ahead before he topped it, and saw the supply train pulling away. He instantly spurred his horse after it, in a race to catch it up, pitting horseflesh against hot steel. Slowly, inch by inch, his horse began gaining ground, galloping with nostrils flaring, with Miller spurring it on to run faster.

Ahead in the engine cab, the fireman turned reaching for another armload of wood, when he saw a horse and rider pounding closer, beginning to pass the last of the loaded flatbeds. Fascinated by the sight, he called out to F.W: 'Would you look at that, Mr Thurston. Some cowboy is racing us!' He pointed back, surprise on his face.

F.W. grabbed the steel door rail, leaning out to get a better look as Miller's galloping horse edged closer. He marvelled at the rider's wild daring and skill, the flying hoofs of his horse a blur of speed.

'He's some rider,' the boss man admitted, a smile coming over his face. 'Maybe he wants a job!'

'A job?' the engineer questioned. 'Not that cowboy, sir. Look how he's dressed, and his horse. He's no gandy dancer.'

Miller drove his horse harder, passing the last flatbed and then riding the horse up on the gravel berm, dangerously close to the steel rails and the bucking, belching locomotive. He reached out and grabbed the door rail, at the same time kicking his feet out of the stirrups, and then pulled himself up inside the engine cab in one quick jump, the engineer and fireman shaking their heads in disbelief as he did so.

'Do you always board a train like that?' F.W. questioned over the roar of the locomotive.

'Not hardly,' Judd shook his head. 'This is the first time I've ever been on a train. You weren't going to stop, so I had no other choice.'

'What about your horse?' Thurston looked back at the still running animal slowly falling behind.

'He'll follow us. It'll just take him a little time to catch up after this thing stops.'

'So, what is your big rush to take a chance like this to get on board?'

'I want to get up to the railhead, and see the boss man, whoever that is.'

'You must have good reason to do so, after all this?'

'I do. I need to find out if plans for the railroad might go through a piece of ground my brother and I own, outside Red Bluffs. He was murdered by someone who might already know that. They tried to do the same to me, too. The only place I can get that answer is from the boss of this railroad.'

The smile on Thurston's face vanished, quickly replaced by a furrowed brow of concern. 'Then I must tell you I am F.W. Thurston, the man you're looking for. I will also say that the only man I've talked to about the area around Red Bluffs is the mayor, Cyrus Toomey.'

'You're the owner of this entire outfit?' Judd pushed his hat back on his head.

'I am, though I might not look like it, standing here covered in black ashes from the smoke stack. And what is your name, sir?'

'It's Judd Miller. I sure didn't expect to meet you like this, but I guess it's as good a way as any.'

'I agree, Mr Miller. We can have a more expansive

conversation once we reach the railhead and my personal car, without having to shout at each other. Enjoy the ride, it's free on me!'

Two days later, F.W. sat in his padded chair, smoking a cigar, while Judd sat across from him, carefully going over the events of the last few months in detail. When he finished, Thurston let out a long sigh of displeasure.

'So, what you're telling me is I'm sitting here listening to all this from a wanted man with a price on his head,' he paused. 'Am I correct?'

'You are, and I am. But from what you've already told me, I now know Cyrus Toomey had to have a hand in what happened to my brother and me. He knew about your plans, and tried to have us both killed, to get his hands on our ranch. Some of what I've done after I fled from my place, I had no choice in doing. I had to defend myself, or die. It was just that simple. Yeah, I've used this six-gun more times than maybe I wanted to, but it was me or the men I had to face. I won't make any excuses for that.'

F.W. stroked his beard, taking a small sip from his brandy snifter, before speaking. 'I've always thought of myself to be a good judge of character. I've had to be, to deal with the men I know in the business world. Your story sounds so improbable, I'm compelled to believe it. I don't think anyone could make it up. This means that any prior dealings I had with Cyrus Toomey are over. He's far more than a mayor. He may even be subject to a criminal investigation for murder. Come over to my map table.' Thurston got to his feet, beckoning Miller to follow.

The large map spread out noted the date and progress of the rail-laying crew, plus a dotted line for the way ahead and the progress expected to be met. F.W. put a finger down tracing the route he'd take when it reached the first high country at Red Bluffs. 'Here is where I must begin the climb up and over the mountains. Does any of this look familiar to you?'

Judd leaned closer, pointing out his ranch property. 'That's my place.' He looked over at Thurston.

'And that is exactly the piece of land I was trying to negotiate with your mayor. I now also know all you've told me is the truth. The only question left is, what you mean to do about it?'

Judd replied, 'The first thing I have to find out is if Toomey or any of his cronies have tried to take my property away from me. He owns the few officials that Red Bluffs has, so he can get away with practically anything. If I can prove the land is still mine, will you deal with me on a sale for your right of way?'

'I will, but exactly how do you intend to accomplish that?'

'I'll have to ride out of here back to my friends and come up with something on the way. How long before you think you'll reach Red Bluffs?'

'At our current rate of laying steel, I'd say it should take another two and a half weeks. Once I get there, I'll either offer a contract to you, or be forced to change plans to take another route into the high country. That choice would be prohibitively costly, and I know my investors would not look favourably upon my doing so. I'd much prefer we can conclude a deal, and for more than just the money end, after what you've told me about all that's happened to you and your brother. There has to be some sense of justice introduced into all this. If you can flush out this mayor of yours for what you believe he might have done, I'll instruct my attorneys to defend you in any sort of legal proceedings about what has happened to you. You know what a good lawyer is worth, don't you?'

'No, I can't say I do.'

'A good lawyer is worth ten men with shotguns. Don't forget that.'

'I appreciate that offer. I'll probably need all the legal help I can get before all this is over. I'll see you in a couple of weeks, in Red Bluffs.'

Both men shook hands, and Thurston walked Judd to the door of his railcar, watching him saddle up and start away. F.W. stroked his beard, while puffing on a thick cigar, and whispered to himself as he turned away to close the door: 'I hope God is riding with you, cowboy. Because no one else will be, and you'll need all the help you can get!'

Miller pushed the tired horse steadily west, reaching the first foothills in four days. Three more brought him to the wagon camp on the ridge, arriving minutes before sundown. Lacey heard the horse coming in first, while Moses sat on the tailgate of his wagon, still nursing the savage dragging he'd taken at the hands of Jared Bass.

'Moses, he's back!' Lacey dropped the armload of firewood she was carrying, as Judd rode in, pulling to a stop with a tired smile on his face. As he eased himself down out of the saddle, she ran up and wrapped both arms around him, burying her head in his chest. 'I'm so glad you're home safe. I couldn't stop worrying about you!' She fought back tears.

The preacher got to his feet with a grunt of pain, a smile spreading across his thin gaunt face, as he came up. 'I prayed hard for you, boy. I knew the Good Lord would watch over you, I knew it.' He clamped both hands around Judd's shoulders.

That evening, eating dinner over a small campfire, Judd explained all he'd learned in his meeting with F.W. Thurston. 'I've got to see if my land deed is still in my name, after all this time, or whether Toomey and his pals have changed it.'

'But how are you going to do that?' Lacey wondered out loud. 'If you show your face in town, they'll have you arrested and thrown in jail, or worse.'

'I've had plenty of time to think about that on my way back here. I'm convinced the only way is for me to go into town at night.'

'That sounds dangerous to me, too.' Moses slowly shook his head.

'It is, but it's the only way I can do what I have to, if I can get some help doing it.'

'Help? Who is going to help a wanted man? The whole town would like to get their hands on that reward money.' The worry in Lacey's voice was obvious.

'The kind of help I'm talking about won't have any choice. Toomey uses a local judge, Westin Carlyle, for all his legal dealings. If anyone knows about my land deed, it's Carlyle. I mean to use him, too.'

'Why would he help you?' Moses questioned.

'He won't have any choice. I'm shall go into town tomorrow night and convince him.'

The ghostly glow of a half moon lit the large, two-storey Carlyle house and the expensive, wrought-iron fence surrounding it, showing up the dark shadow of Judd Miller as he eased over the backyard fence and quietly made his way up to the tall building. A wooden latticework stood against the house, woven with thick climbing vines. Miller tested it for steadiness, before carefully beginning a slow climb up to the second-floor balcony.

Reaching it, he climbed over the porch rail, stopping a moment to catch his breath, surveying double doors leading inside. At the door he tested the knob with a firm twist. It did not budge. He tried a second time with both hands. Still it did not give. Lifting his six-gun from its holster, he gripped it by the barrel and used the pistol grip as a hammer, striking the door glass in short, quick strokes until it broke. Reaching inside, he found the key still in the lock. One twist and he stepped inside.

Instead of the bedroom he expected, he found himself in a large study and office. Crossing the room to a second door, he eased it slowly open, revealing a large bedroom with a four-poster bed against the far wall. Covered in thick blankets up to his neck lay Westin Carlyle, snoring peacefully in his fancy night-cap, his silver white hair sticking out from under the cap. Judd stepped to the bed, the pistol still in his hands, levelling the cold steel barrel against Carlyle's exposed neck.

'Wake up!' he whispered in a low, firm voice.

Carlyle mumbled something, trying to push away the annoying object pressing against his neck.

'I said, wake up!' Miller yanked the cap off Carlyle's head, grabbing him by his nightshirt and pulling him upright into a sitting position, his eyes still closed, struggling to realize what was happening to him.

'What . . . who . . . is it?' He rubbed his eyes open, trying to focus in the dimly lit room.

'Listen to me, you old crook. You're going with me downtown to your office. Wake up and get some clothes on, or I'll drag you there in your nightshirt!'

Westin blinked hard, trying to make some sense of what was happening to him, and who was doing it. Judd pulled him closer, face to face, until he realized who it was.

'Miller . . . I thought you were . . . dead. Have you gone crazy? They'll hang you for this, too.'

'I said, get up and get some clothes on!' He dragged the old man to his feet. 'You and I are going to take a close look at my land deed. Get moving!'

'You mean the deed to your property?'

'That's exactly what I mean. Start dressing.'

'We don't have to go to my office down town.'

115

'What do you mean by that?'

'I keep things like that right here in my home, in the next room.'

Judd lit the coal oil lamp and sat it on the office desk, while Carlyle knelt in front of a big black wheel-safe, slowly twisting the combination on its dial until the tumblers clicked and the heavy steel door swung open. He brought up a large, flat steel box, and laid it on the desk. Opening the lid, he shuffled through a sheaf of papers, finally coming up with the Miller land deed, reading it a moment before handing it to Judd.

'I'm afraid . . . you don't own this piece of property any more,' he hesitated, staring at Judd with fear in his eyes.

'What do you mean, I don't own my own ranchland?'

He shoved Carlyle into a chair behind the desk, reading it for himself. His name and his brother Randall had been crossed out on the title, and Cyprus Toomey's name was handwritten in above it. Judd looked up with fire in his eyes.

'You get a piece of paper and that pen and inkwell. You're going to write down that the original land deed is valid, and Toomey's name is a fraud, put there by you. Date it today, so there's no question when you amended it.'

Westin stared back, swallowing just once as his face dropped and his mouth opened to speak. 'But . . . I could be jailed for forgery and fraud, tampering with an official document like this. I'd lose my judgeship

116

. . . I'd be disbarred.'

Judd levelled the six-gun, pushing the barrel hard against Carlyle's chest, as he leaned down face to face with the white-haired man. 'You'll never get that far, if you don't start writing right now. I've killed more than one man. One more won't make any difference now.'

Westin picked up the pen and dipped it in the inkwell, but his hand was shaking so badly he couldn't begin to write. 'I need a drink of bourbon, to steady myself.' He nodded towards a fancy glass decanter on the end of the desk, next to a silver glass holder. Judd pulled it over and watched as Carlyle poured bourbon into the stubby glass to the rim, and tipped it up in one quick motion.

'All right, now that you've got yourself some back-bone, start writing,' Miller ordered.

The judge carefully wrote in the new addendum to the deed, all the while beads of nervous perspiration breaking out on his lined face. When he had finished, he sank back in the chair, a defeated man who knew that his career, position and wealth had been suddenly ended, and by his own hand.

'I suppose you know that what I've done here means I'm going to end up in jail?' He looked up at Judd's stare. 'I'm too old to serve time. I'd die in a prison.'

'You should have thought of that before you threw in with Toomey. You knew what he was, just like everyone else around here. If you're looking for sympathy, forget it. I lost my brother because of you and

117

him. I'm taking Toomey and Bass down next.'

'I had nothing to do with that killing.'

'The hell you didn't. This land swindle you helped start was exactly why Randall was killed, and you helped pull the trigger. If they hang you along with the others, I couldn't care less. Now you can go run to him and tell him what you've done here. But he won't be your partner for two seconds, when you do. He'll cut you loose to fend for yourself, or have Bass come in here and take care of you his way. Whatever happens, you've earned it.'

Judd rolled up the deed in a tight cylinder, slipping it inside his jacket and holstering his six-gun. Crossing the room he opened the double doors, disappearing down the trellis, leaving Westin Carlyle sitting at his desk. He turned out the lamp and lowered his head into both hands, wondering what to do next.

Jared Bass was finally back on his feet, as he stepped into Cyrus Toomey's office, ready to go back to work and do his boss's bidding.

'I'm glad to see you up and around,' Toomey greeted him as he approached his desk. 'The first thing I want you to do, is get over to Carlyle's house and tell him I want the Miller land deed he keeps in his safe. The railroad should be coming closer by now, and I want it in my hands to start dealing with this F.W. Thurston, who runs the whole thing.'

Just twenty minutes later, Bass burst back into Toomey's office. 'You ain't gonna believe this!' he almost shouted.

'Believe what?'

'The judge has hung himself! He's dead! I found him strung up from a roof beam in his bedroom, and this note was tucked into his pyjama pocket!' He handed it to Toomey, who was too stunned even to speak for a moment, as he unfolded the small piece of paper and began reading it:

Cyrus. This dangerous game we've been playing is over. Judd Miller knows all about it. I won't be put in a jail cell to rot what few years I have left to me. You're on your own, now. Goodbye.

'Miller is back here in town!' The mayor's voice suddenly rose to a sinister shout, as he jumped up from behind his desk. 'You find him and kill him! Not like the last time when you thought the desert did the job for you! And now you don't have to wonder any more who bushwhacked you and horse dragged you up and down the street, either. Get out of here and do what I say, or we'll all swing together!'

CHAPTER NINE

Back in the ridgeline camp, Judd pulled the deed out of his jacket and showed it to Lacey and Moses, without opening it.

'You sure got what you needed, to flush out this mayor and his pals,' Moses nodded with a thin smile.

'Yes, but it also did one other thing,' Judd admitted.

'What's that?' Lacey asked.

'Toomey and his friends now know I'm back here, and that means they'll be riding all over the country trying to find me. Sooner or later they'll show up here, and that puts you two in real danger. I can't let that happen. I want both of you to pack and leave here early tomorrow morning. I'll draw you a map of how to get down out of this country into the prairie, and directions to Thurston's track-laying crews.'

'No, I won't go. Don't ask me to do that, Judd!' Lacey's sudden outburst of emotion caught both men off guard. 'I'm not going to see another man I love taken away from me. I won't do it!' She shook with emotion.

Judd grabbed her by both shoulders, pulling her face to face. 'Listen to me, Lacey. You have to go. You and Moses must get this deed to Thurston. He'll buy my property. He's already told me so. And there's one other thing I wasn't going to tell you, but now I have to. I had Carlyle put your name on the deed next to mine. If something does happen to me, at least I'll know you'll be able to sell it to the railroad, and make some real money from it. You'd be able to do anything you want, go anyplace you'd like to. You can't do that by staying here. Everything I've done would be for nothing. Now do you understand why you have to go?'

She pushed her head into Judd's chest, her eyes brimming with hot tears, trying to choke out a question. 'What good would all this do . . . if I didn't have you to do it with?'

'At least I'd know you had the land, and no one else could ever get their hands on it. That's everything to me.' Judd looked to Moses, standing near by. 'You understand what I'm saying, don't you?'

The preacher nodded before speaking. 'I don't like the idea of you taking on Toomey and his men by yourself. I know how good you are with that cross-draw six-gun, but that's long odds, Judd. I'd like to stay and help out, you have to know that. All I can do is pray for you if we leave. It worked pretty well before, so maybe it will again, if I haven't worn out my welcome with the Lord.'

'I want both of you out of here first thing in the

121

morning. When I'm finished with Toomey and anyone else, I'll ride for the railhead, and meet you there. I just don't know how long that might take.'

Judd knew his words were a tall promise he might not be able to keep. But for Lacey's sake he hoped it sounded positive. The look on Moses' face said that he understood that too, without saying so.

Dawn was only a thin grey slash in the eastern sky when the wagon started away down the ridge, with Lacey leaning out looking back, waving goodbye. Judd raised his hand, a thin smile on his lips. Once the wagon went out of sight, he scattered the fire-pit stones, cleaning up the camp of any debris that might show how recently they'd been there. He expected Jared Bass would be the deputy that Toomey would use to try and find him, plus any other gun hands the mayor might be able to hire. Miller knew Moses was right, when he said long odds were against him. But he also knew that the best way to reduce those odds was by taking on Toomey's men under the cover of darkness. Night-time was now his friend: it helped even the score. He'd use every minute of it to his advantage, until dawn lit the land again and he faded out of sight like a disappearing shadow.

Late that afternoon a forbidding, blood-red sun sank into a crimson-backed sky, as if foretelling that death was coming to someone in Red Bluffs, once again. Judd had stayed out of town all that day, hiding in the hills, but by night he could still see the distant glow of street lamps and the dark contour of buildings. As he watched, a sudden flare of lit torches danced like so many fireflies, while riders gathered on the street under orders from Jared Bass, to search for him. A few moments later, the posse rode out of town until their flaming clubs were lost from sight in thick timber.

Now Miller had exactly what he wanted: the vigilantes gone, and an opportunity for him to ride in under cover of darkness. An hour later he got to a side street where he hitched his horse to a rail in an alley; he then made his way on foot to the back door of Cyrus Toomey's office, facing Main Street. The door was locked, as he expected, but quick work using the thin blade on his pocket knife, and the lock clicked open. He stepped into the darkened office, closing the door behind him. The dim light of street lamps outside barely lit the office through curtained windows, as he made his way over to a large oak desk in the centre of the room. Sitting in a big, leather-padded chair, he pulled at the desk drawer. It was locked. A silver-bladed letter opener lay on the desk. Judd reached for it, inserting it in the drawer lock – a quick jimmying job, and the drawer pulled open.

Two large, leather-bound ledgers lay inside on top of a thick sheaf of papers. He pulled up the first book, opened it, and tried to read it in the poor light – but he couldn't. He lit a match from the ornate match holder on the desk, holding it up to the first page, reading as much as he could before it burned out. This brief scan down the page revealed rows of various entries in dollars made by many of the businesses in town, to Toomey's personal account. Miller took them to be pay-off money of some kind. He closed the ledger, and pulled up the second one, opening it in the light of a newly flaring matchstick. This one showed line after written line of plans about the railroad coming closer, along with the names of people and the events they would become involved with, in association with it. Near the bottom of the third page he saw his brother's name alongside Rachel Toomey's, both underlined in two dark slashes of ink; then the second match burned out.

Judd pushed back in the chair. Closing his eyes for a moment, he realized what he had. These records were invaluable. They could end up putting Cyrus Toomey in jail for a long time, or possibly even seeing him mount a gallows.

Suddenly outside he heard the sound of many horses returning, pulling to a halt. Jared Bass's loud voice quickly followed. 'I want everyone back here tomorrow at nine o'clock. This night riding is a little hard on everyone, but I thought we'd try it first, and might catch Miller quick. Anyone who don't show up will answer to Mayor Toomey. You all know what that means, don't you? Now, get out of here!'

Judd crossed the room, easing back from the curtain to see Bass still standing there, watching the men ride away, with his hands on his hips. As he turned to start up the street to the Rough and Ready, for a drink to wash down the night's frustration and failure, Judd quickly opened the front door and stepped out on the boardwalk.

'You been looking for me?' Miller stepped out on to the street, as Bass spun on his heels, staring wide-eyed at the dark shadow of the man twenty feet away.

'Who . . . who is it?' His voice caught with emotion, already fearing that he knew that voice.

'It's me, Judd Miller, you back-shooting bastard. Now sundown is going to set on you twice, and for the last time!'

Bass's heart skipped a beat, and his breath caught in his throat as his stomach tightened in knots. He froze, not daring to make any move, lifting his hands belt high.

'It was Toomey ordered all that . . . don't blame me for any of it. I was just following orders, I swear it.'

'You remember being rope dragged up and down this street, don't you?' Jared nodded, but did not answer. 'Now you don't have to wonder who did it to you.'

Bass fought for something to say, anything to hold off Miller's anger, and what he meant to do about it. 'You . . . you better not make any more trouble for yourself than you're already into, you gotta know that.'

'Trouble? You're in it up to your ears. So is Toomey. I'm taking him down after I'm done with you. But before I pull on you, I want just one question answered.'

'What . . . question, what are you talking about?'

'Are you the one who killed my brother Randall?'

'Now wait a minute . . . we were all acting under

Toomey's orders. We only meant to scare him off into selling your place. But he pulled a pistol, and starting shooting at us. I don't know who got a bullet into him. It could have been anybody. Nobody knows. It was dark, just like this . . . no one can say for sure.'

'Yeah, it was dark like this. I've waited a long time to catch up to you. You're going to pay for what you've done, not only to my brother and me, but other people around this town who've been run off or found dead. Your time is up, Bass. Go ahead and pull it!'

'I aint' gonna pull on you. I wouldn't stand a chance!'

'Then I'll kill you where you stand. I said, pull it!'

Bass fumbled for the pistol, finally clearing its holster, but he was already a dead man. Judd's six-gun spit fire and thunder once, twice, the impact of the bullets driving Bass backwards until he fell to the ground, rolling over on his face moaning once, before quivering in death.

Judd ran back into the office, closing the door and locking it behind him. He stopped at the desk only long enough to ink a short note:

You're next. Get ready for it, Toomey!

A crowd of men were milling about in the street next morning in front of the mayor's office, when he rode up in his one-horse buggy. He already knew Jared Bass had been killed the previous evening, and who the one man was that likely did the shooting.

Toomey was scared, although he tried not to show it. If Judd Miller had gotten this bold and close, there was nothing he wouldn't do to get to him, too. Cyrus knew the only way he could survive was if somehow he could get someone else to kill Miller. His own life depended on it. He'd tried to have Miller killed twice, and both times had failed.

The throng of men shouted questions as he pulled the buggy to a stop, but instead of getting down, he stood from the seat, eyeing all those around him. This was it: it was now or never: he had to come up with something that would finish off this cowboy once and for all.

'Miller did kill Jared, last night, didn't he?' One man shouted.

'Of course, who else but a mad-dog killer would do something like that, right here on our own main street!' Toomey shouted back, shaking his fist in the air. 'And I'll tell all of you something else, too. If Miller isn't found and hung, there won't be a safe street anywhere in this town where decent people can walk the streets without fear of the same thing happening to them. Like any rabid animal, there's only one way to deal with him. He has to be hunted down and shot on sight! To that end, I'm personally offering two thousand dollars of my own money to the man who gets a bullet in him!'

'With Bass dead, who is the new town sheriff?' Another bystander called out.

'It looks like that has to be me, until I can find someone else to take on the job. I'm going to deputize

127

myself, soon as I get into my office. If Miller tries coming back here, we'll get up a quick rope party, and swing him right here on the street. Now listen to me, all of you. I want you to go back home and get your pistols and shotguns loaded. We'll make Red Bluffs into an armed camp that no one in their right mind would try to come into. When you're walking the streets, keep them handy. If you want to come out at night and do the same thing, that's all right, too. Just remember that two thousand dollars I'm putting up. The first man to collect it will be rich!'

After inciting the crowd to violence, Toomey unlocked the door and stepped into his office. The first thing he saw was the note on his desk. Picking it up, he read the terse few words, then quickly crumpled it in his hand, throwing it back down on the desk as if it were a hot poker. Not only had Miller killed Bass, now he'd also been right here in his own office. The hair on the back of his neck tingled with fear, and his face flushed red. He saw the desk drawer was ajar, and his silver letter opener nearby. Walking round the desk he was almost afraid to pull it all the way open – but when he did, he found his ledger books gone. Fear gripped him a second time. If those records were ever made public, he could face charges of embezzlement, falsifying public records, and even plotting murder.

He sat down and lowered his head in one hand while beating on the desk with the other. Fighting to gain control of himself, he finally straightened up, scooping up the remaining papers. Getting up, he went across the room to the safe and knelt in front of it, working the shiny silver dial back and forth until the heavy steel door swung open. From inside he extracted a large, flat metal box, and took it back to the desk. Opening it, he lifted out rows of neatly wrapped large bills, along with two bulging leather pouches filled with gold and silver coins. If Miller could come into town and do what he did, Toomey could not take the chance that he might come again and this time blow the safe, getting every last dirty dollar Cyrus had to his name.

The only thing left to do was take everything back to his house on the opposite end of the same street Carlyle had lived on. He could lock himself in the big, rambling mansion until Judd was caught, jailed or killed. His daughter Rachel was back east visiting relatives, and he wasn't sure when she'd return. He had the scabrous home all to himself, and enough weapons to stand off an army. At least it was a plan that made some sense and might work. He shoved everything into a large cloth case and headed for the door, and his buggy.

Judd had retreated far enough back into the mountains from town, to be certain no one could follow him there. It was the old hunting camp once used by himself and his brother Randall and just being here brought back fond memories of the days when they had hunted deer and elk together, and had then sat by a crackling, evening campfire, eating delicious and tender backstrap, roasted on sticks. The glow of

129

those memories didn't last long. He had these damning records of Toomey's in his saddle-bags, but knew they could not stay there. If he was caught or, worse, killed, he'd have risked all this for nothing. He had to find a safe place to hide them until they could be needed in court.

At the back of the old hunting camp, surrounded by tall, white bark quaking aspen, a rocky cliff rose nearly straight up for several hundred feet. Its rocky face was scarred with cracks and crevices, and one larger fissure caught his eye half way up, under an overhanging lip. He retrieved the ledgers from his saddle-bags, wrapping them in his rain slicker, and slowly began to scale the slippery stone wall. His hard-heeled boots slipped and scraped off the rock as he struggled to pull himself higher, inch by inch, until finally he reached the hollowed-out shelf. Reaching in with one hand, he cleaned out the duff of an old hawk's nest, then slid the packet as far as his arms could reach until it stopped at the back.

Satisfied it was safe from the weather, Judd slowly lowered himself back down to the ground. Looking up, he was certain no one would have a prayer of finding it but him. After spending three more days in camp, he decided Toomey had had enough time to worry and to wonder what he'd do next. It was time to saddle up and ride for Red Bluffs, and finish what he'd started.

Cyrus Toomey had spent sleepless nights and fear-filled days, literally barricaded in his house. Judd's promise to get him haunted his every waking moment. He refused to leave the big home for any reason, and at night tip-toed from one window to the next, peeking out behind curtains, searching for the shadowed figure of Judd Miller stalking closer. Every night sound, every creak and groan of the house, set Toomey off on another sweat-soaked moment of abject fear, pulling both pistols he'd stuck in his pants top, for protection.

He finally collapsed in his chair, four nights later, and had just fallen asleep when an incessant knocking on the front door caused him to leap straight up out of the chair, pulling both pistols, eyes wide in terror. He started to flee up the stairs to the bedrooms, when the muffled voice of his daughter Rachel calling out stopped him. Creeping to the door, he lit the coal oil lamp on the table next to it, pulling one pistol, and kicking aside the chair he'd used to wedge under the doorknob.

'Who . . . is it?' he called out, lifting the .22-calibre revolver, belt high.

'Daddy, it's me, Rachel. Open the door.'

Cyrus undid the double locks on the big door, slowly opening it just far enough for him to peek out. The glow of the table lantern lit his daughter's pretty face and the cascading curls of black hair down to her shoulders, and the suitcase held in one hand.

'What are you doing, why are you holding a gun?' she questioned, pushing the door open, walking inside, before he quickly slammed it shut again, propping the chair back up under the handle and slamming both locks shut.

'Daddy, what's happened here, you look terrible?' She looked him up and down.

He grabbed her by one hand, lamp in the other, and pulled her into the parlour.

'Did you see anyone when you came up?' he demanded, wide eyed.

'See anyone, what do you mean? The buggy driver dropped me off, if that's what you mean?'

'No, no, I mean someone like Judd Miller.'

'Judd Miller? I thought you told me he'd been killed. Are you saying he's now alive?'

'Yes, he's alive, and he's already come back here and shot down Jared Bass, in cold blood. He even forced Westin Carlyle to hang himself. Now he's vowed to kill me, too. I've been up day and night trying to stop him!'

Rachel lowered the suitcase, staring at her father. Clearly he was at his wits end.

'How long have you been living like this?' She asked.

'I'm not sure any more. Maybe four or five days. Miller wants to kill me because he thinks I had some-thing to do with his brother's death. He's gone stark raving mad about it. Now that you're back in town, we've both got to leave. Do you understand why I've had to live like this?'

The thought of Randall Miller made Rachel pause a moment. She had deeply loved the handsome young man, and his sudden death by unknown assas-sins still haunted her, and all the questions that went with it – including her original questions to her father, right after it happened. Now all the pain, suspicions and questions she'd buried came rushing back.

'Why is Judd Miller so sure you had a hand in Randall's death?

'Who knows? He's gone mad, killing anyone who gets in his way. You can't reason with an insane killer like that. He has to blame someone, so he blames me. Who knows why!'

Rachel took in a deep breath. Her shoulders dropped from fatigue, tired from the long stage ride, and now all this. 'I've got to get some sleep. In the morning, I'll see if I can get some of your business friends to help you. I'm sure someone will. Maybe we can hire some men to protect you. Let's both get some rest. You certainly need it too.'

'I'm not going to bed. I can't sleep. I'm staying right down here in the parlour, where I can watch the door and windows. I'm not going to have my throat cut while I'm asleep, not on your life!'

'Daddy, I knew Judd Miller well enough when I was going out with Randall. I just can't believe he'd come here and do something like this.'

'Believe what you want. I'm telling you he's gone mad. He even broke into my office, and stole personal papers of mine. Then he left a note on my desk, saying I was next to be killed after Bass!'

'Will you please come upstairs, and try to get some sleep? You're a nervous wreck like this. Judd Miller isn't going to come here and try anything like that.

133

In the shape you're in, you might end up shooting yourself. Do it for me, please?'

'I can't. You go ahead. I'm staying right here with my pistol!'

Rachel stared at her father for only a moment before she gave up, and turned for the stairs and her bedroom. Maybe in the morning she would be able to talk some sense into him.

CHAPTER TEN

Toomey collapsed into a big, plush parlour chair, struggling to stay awake, driven by sweat-soaked fear, the pistol still gripped tightly in his hands. He turned the lantern down low, on the table next to him. For another half hour he fought off increasingly leaden eyelids that begged to close. Twenty more minutes and his head slowly began to droop toward his chest. One last time he was able to fight off the overpowering urge to sleep, but the next, he lost the battle, going limp in the chair. Exhaustion and fear won.

The gold-cased clock on the fireplace mantel monotonously ticked away the seconds, and the minutes, and finally another hour, its tiny bell ringing eleven o'clock. Toomey lay mouth open, lost in deep sleep, while the shadow of a man silently eased over the backyard fence and up to the tall, dark structure. No one heard the double French door lock give way to the twist of a sturdy belt knife, so the man could slip inside. Crossing the room he made his way to another door. Opening it led to a long, dark hallway leading to the parlour. A dim glow of light lit his way. Reaching it, six-gun in hand, he saw Cyrus Toomey collapsed in a chair, snoring loudly.

Silently crossing the room he stopped in front of the chair, looking down on the man who had so drastically changed the course of his life into running from the law to stay free, deadly gunfights, and Wanted posters promising to hang him if ever he were caught. Ever so slowly he reached down and eased the little revolver from out of Toomey's limp hand, tucking it into his belt. Now he was ready to extract the sweet vengeance he'd waited for and dreamed of for so long.

'Wake up!' he shouted, grabbing the little man by his shirt collar, dragging him up to his feet. Cyrus's bloodshot eyes flickered open, trying to make some sense of what was happening to him. He staggered, unsteady on his feet, rubbing the sleep out of his eyes with both hands, suddenly facing the man he'd dreaded seeing more than lingering death itself.

'Miller . . . Miller . . . don't kill me. I'm begging you . . . put that six-gun down. It was . . . Bass, did all the killing, not me. I swear to God, it wasn't me!'

Up in her bedroom, Rachel woke to the sound of her father's terrified shout. She hurriedly put on her robe, and quickly descended the stairs. At the bottom she stopped for a moment, staring unbelievingly at the sight of both men.

'Judd, what are you doing here? Put down that revolver!' She crossed the room, as Miller held up his hand ordering her to stay back.

'You stay out of this, Rachel. It's between me and your father, if you can call him that. He's as cold-blooded a bastard as the men he paid to murder my brother and me. Now he's going to pay for it!'

'A cold-blooded murderer? And you believe pulling that trigger doesn't make you one, too? Think about what you're doing, while you still can. Stop this right now!'

She boldly shoved Judd back, forcing her way between the two men. Cyrus grabbed her from behind with both hands, pulling her up against him, shielding himself shamelessly.

'Get out of here, Rachel. I've waited too long for this!' Judd tried pushing her aside.

'No, I won't. You want to kill someone so badly, go ahead and shoot, because you're going to have to kill me too, to do it!' Her voice rose to an emotional challenge.

'He killed my brother, and the man you loved and planned to marry. Have you forgotten about that? Is it so easy for you to do now?'

'No, I haven't forgotten. But I know that you pulling that trigger won't bring Randall back, and you know it too. Get out of here or you'll be on the run for murder and will regret it for the rest of your life. I'm not going to stand here and watch you become judge, jury and executioner. If you loved your brother as much as I did, and still do, you won't dirty his name and memory by doing this. Don't, Judd. It's wrong and you know it is!'

137

Miller's eyes bored into the defiant young woman while she stared back without blinking. He knew she wasn't going to move. The six-gun in his hand was still levelled waist high. Tense seconds passed as Rachel's words sank in. Judd finally swallowed as if he was going to speak, but instead he took in a long, slow breath, then slowly lowered the revolver and holstered it. He struggled to keep his voice level from the rage of emotion churning inside him.

'He's going to pay for what he's done, and you can't stop it. I'm going to see to it, if it's the last thing I do. You can't protect him forever. I've got the proof I need in two ledgers, to put him behind bars or see a hangman's rope.'

'Then maybe a court will settle it. Haven't you had enough killing using that six-gun of yours for answers?'

'Maybe I have. But I didn't start out this way, remember? All Randall and I wanted was to build our ranch, until your father and his crooked pals stepped in. He is the cause of everything that happened after that to me, you and everyone else.'

Judd stepped back, never taking his eyes off her, until he turned for the front door. Letting himself out, he disappeared into the cold starry night without another word, noticing for the first time that he was shivering with emotion. He'd come to kill Toomey, and now Rachel had suddenly stopped him. Why had he let her, he wondered to himself, after all his plans to get even. Was he losing the bitter edge of vengeance that he'd sworn to uphold. The only thing left that he was still certain of, was that if he couldn't do it with a six-gun, he'd finish Toomey in a court of law. It could not end like this.

Rachel went to the door and closed it, while Cyrus collapsed back in the chair, burying his head in both hands, his shoulders shaking. She returned and stood silently behind him for a moment, summoning all the strength she had for what she was about to say.

'I always wondered if you had anything to do with Randall's death. Now maybe I'll finally have to find out. If you did, Father, I'll never speak another word to you, ever again. Do you understand me?'

He struggled to his feet, reaching out to grab her, but she pushed his hands away, starting across the room for the stairs – but she stopped before going up, and said 'Tomorrow I'm going to pack my things and move out, until all this is over. I can no longer live here in this house with you, until I get some answers. I don't have to explain why, after all this, do I?'

'Wait, Rachel . . . I can explain everything. You have to believe me. None of this happened the way Miller says it did! He's half crazy. You saw it. He meant to kill me!'

She turned away and made her way up the stairs, until the bedroom door closed behind her, leaving Cyrus Toomey standing there staring after her, still pleading to be heard, and lying to save himself.

After leaving the Toomey house, Judd moved quickly.

He knew Cyrus might try anything now. If he decided to run for it, it could take months or even years to catch up with him, if ever. He rode fast out of town and headed for the old hunting camp to pick up the ledgers he'd secreted there in the rock wall. He had to retrieve them, ride for the railroad and Thurston, and get the papers to the lawyers F.W. had promised he'd use against Toomey, if Judd could bring him proof. Judd meant to test that offer.

Miller had been right about Toomey's reaction. Once the trembling fear of being executed had worn off, he quickly began taking stock of what options he had to keep that confrontation from happening twice. The answer always came up the same, and that was to kill Miller any way he could. The following morning Cyrus watched as Rachel marched out of the front door looking straight ahead and carrying two cloth clothing bags filled with her personal belongings. She neither looked at him, nor spoke a single word. After the door slammed shut behind her, he quickly went upstairs to dress and walk down to Main Street one block away. He had a new idea that might work to save himself.

The first saloon he came to, he pushed through the front door. Inside a dozen early drinkers were already at the bar, who turned to see who had come in. 'Well, I'll be damned!' Mike Gilles, owner of the Dry Mouth saloon, turned with a look of surprise on his face. 'This is the first time I've ever seen you in here. I think I'll give you one on the house, just for the hell of it!'

'I'm not here to drink the swill you serve up. I'm here because last night that murdering coward, Judd Miller, broke into my house and tried to kill me! Most of you men know that just a days ago I offered any man, or men, two thousand dollars to run him down and kill him. Not one man responded. Now I'm upping that to three thousand dollars, and I don't care how it's done. Even if three or four men get together and do the job, that's still a lot of money to split among them. I say, saddle up and find Miller. It's open season on him. When he's dead, there'll be no questions asked by me or anyone else how it was done, or by who. Is there anyone in here with enough stones to take on the job? Speak up!'

Gilles looked at his customers leaning on the bar, and waited for a reply. No one uttered a word. Looking back to Toomey, he gave him an answer of his own: 'Mr Mayor, let me tell you something that might save you a lot of time and money. There isn't a man in Red Bluffs who will ride out after Judd Miller. He took down your top gun, Jared Bass, right out here on the street in front of my place, not to mention what the judge did to himself because of Miller. No one is going to out pull him, and he knows it. So does everyone else around here. You could offer four, five, or six thousand dollars. It won't do no good. And I'd have to add, I'm a little surprised that the mayor of this town would come in here and even ask men to kill for him. All of a sudden you don't sound much like a mayor, but more like a hangman.'

'I've been driven to do this because of that rabid

141

animal. He has to be stopped. And if none of you will, mark my words, he'll come back here any time he pleases, and shoot down anyone who opposes him. Whether it's men, women or children, won't make any difference. Is there not even one of you who will do something about it?'

The drinkers only stared back, still in silence, until Gilles spoke up again. 'Well, it looks like if you want Miller dead, you're the one who is going to have to do it yourself. There are no takers in here, or I'd guess anyplace else around town.'

Toomey turned, red-faced, glaring back at the men before leaving the saloon, the fear of desperation beginning to slowly crawl up the back of his neck again. Reaching his house, Cyrus went in checking every door and window, locking himself inside – but it wasn't enough to tamp down the crushing fear that Judd Miller would return and this time finish what he'd started before Rachel stopped him. Now Rachel was gone, and she wasn't coming back – and everyone else who had protected him was dead.

All that long afternoon he paced the floor, pistol in his hand, trying to decide what to do next. No place in Red Bluffs was safe, not even here in his own home. With shaking hands he poured himself a stiff drink of rye whiskey from the glass decanter on the table, sitting down with sweat beading his lined face. There had to be some way out – and suddenly that word 'out' gave him the answer he'd struggled to come up with. He had to get completely out of town fast, and as far away as possible – so far that neither

Judd Miller, nor anyone else, would ever be able to track him down.

He leaped to his feet, hurrying up the stairs to his bedroom, and began to pack as little as possible, in a large cloth travelling bag. When he had finished, he went to the wall safe and took out all the cash he'd retrieved earlier from his office, stuffing some in his pockets and the rest in the bag.

Back downstairs he stood behind a curtained window, watching the sun slowly go down until early evening shadows crept up the street outside. Edging out of the front door, he hurried back to Main Street and the Alexander & Banning stagecoach office. Stepping inside, he found the small waiting room empty, except for the clerk, Harley Tuttle, at the counter, going over paperwork. Tuttle looked up through wire-rimmed glasses. The surprise on his face obvious.

'Why, hello Mr Mayor!' He forced a small smile. 'What brings you here at this hour, sir?'

'I want to know if there's another stage due out of here tonight?'

'Ah, yes there is. The last one should be in for the final run to Canyon City, in about one hour, if they're on time. Why do you ask?'

'Because I'm going to be on it. How much for a ticket?'

Tuttle stared back. It took a moment for him to recover from such a surprising request. 'Well, would it be just for you, or do you have freight of any kind, too?'

143

'No, just for me, and this clothing bag.'

'I see . . . we can put that on top along with other gear.'

'No. I want it inside the coach with me. I don't want it on top of anything.'

'If you insist. I suppose you want a round trip ticket?'

'I do not. Make it one way. And the stage does run further west, doesn't it?'

'Yes sir, it does. How much further west are you considering going?'

'Never mind that. Just mark up my ticket for Canyon City.'

'That'll be twenty dollars, sir. Do you mean to wait here for the stage to come in?'

'Yes, I'll stay right here. I just hope that whip man is on time.'

Later that evening a scimitar-like crescent moon slowly carved its way across a starry night-time sky, while the A & B coach rocked and rattled its way down the narrow mountain road west towards Canyon City, with just one passenger.

Judd Miller rode under that same thin moon but in the opposite direction, east, heading for the rail-head and Thurston's promise of legal help to finish off Cyrus Toomey in a court of law, instead of his own justice with his fast six-gun spitting fire, lead and vengeance. It was a race that one of them had to win, and neither could afford to lose.

Somewhere far ahead, Farris Whitmore Thurston

stepped outside his private railcar, lighting a cigar to the flare of a match, slowly blowing out a big puff of smoke. In these few quiet moments, his mind began replaying all the wild events of recent weeks, and his chance meeting with the strong-willed cowboy, whose story fascinated him endlessly. Now he'd heard even more from Lacey and Moses, who had used Judd's hand-drawn map to find the railroad magnate and spill out their story of what Judd was trying to do next, plus give him the deed records. After a sumptuous dinner cooked by F.W.'s private chef, and the long, evening conversation that followed, Thurston had offered both of them two spare bedrooms at the other end of his railcar, where they'd turned in for the night.

But Thurston could not sleep. He had too much on his mind. Besides, he did some of his best thinking alone at night. He knew Miller was out there riding fast to reach him with the damning personal records that Lacey and the tall preacher had told him about. Since he'd last seen Judd, his rail gang had forged their way further west, mile by back-breaking mile, to the ring of spike mauls laying down more shining steel rails over rough-hewn wooden ties. He took in another long, slow, deep puff of the cigar, blowing it out, stroking his thick beard, whispering to himself once again as he often did.

'If you're out there, cowboy, ride fast and don't stop. Time is of the essence, for both you and me. Neither of us have much of it to spare.'

His unheard wish was being answered, as the dim

145

shadow of horse and rider made its way across tall
prairie grass, Judd Miller pushing his tired horse at a
steady pace east where a new sun would rise. But that
light was still hours away. For now, the stars and a
gentle east wind were his only guides, and he followed them without question.

Six exhausting days and nights later, the unmoving
image of that same horse and rider stood out on a
low rise, as a new sun lit the endless sea of grass in a
golden hue. The pair seemed bronze statues, for
neither moved. Judd had finally given in to the overwhelming urge to stop and sleep. Head down,
leaning forward on the saddle horn, he'd fought off
the constantly increasing demand until he no longer
could, and had finally fallen asleep. He dreamed in
wild images, until the tiny sound of something far
away kept interrupting him. At first it seemed a
distant shriek he could not recognize, and he
mumbled under his breath for it to go away. But it
came back again, this time more whistle than wind.

It moved him to struggle out of his dark world of
sleep, slowly straightening up in the saddle, forcing
his bloodshot eyes to open. Peering through dark
slits, he tried to focus on the world around him.
Nothing but blue sky, wind and grass surrounded
him. He rubbed aching eyes with both hands and
tried again. Far off to the northwest, he thought he
made out a tiny tendril of black smoke curling slowly
up on the horizon. Reaching around behind him he
pulled up a canteen. Opening it, he poured water in

one hand, splashing it across his face. When he looked again, the smoke column rose higher, followed by the whistle of a steel locomotive. Judd Miller had finally found the railhead at last!

F.W. was standing on a flatbed railcar ahead of his personal car, ready to begin another new day laying steel rails. The Chinese work gang hauled long, heavy steel rails past him using rail tongs – eight pig-tailed men opposite each other, straining their backs at Y-shaped tongs hooked under the lip of the rail. Behind Thurston's private car a wood-burning engine had the boiler gauge up, as more black smoke billowed out of its bell-shaped stack. F.W. raised his hand to speak, ready to order his men to start, when he suddenly spied the tiny image of what looked like a horse and rider slowly approaching. He shaded his eyes with both hands, trying to get a clearer view, as the rider came closer. Now he recognized that image: it was Judd Miller! Thurston turned to the engineer, signalling to him to blow the whistle again and again as he pumped his arm in unison, the loud blast drowning out every other sound.

Inside Thurston's fancy railcar, eating breakfast, Lacey and Moses heard the commotion, then saw F.W. leap off the flatbed, before seeing why, as Judd rode in. They both jumped to their feet and rushed out of the door and down the steps, running to meet the cowboy reining to a stop, calling for help to get him down. Farris yelled for men to help him until a dozen hands reached up and Judd collapsed into them.

147

'By God, I knew if anyone could do it, it would be you!' Thurston shouted, pulling Judds' arm over his shoulder, helping to support him to stand up.

'My . . . saddle-bags,' Judd barely got the words out. 'The ledgers are . . . in there.'

'Get this man into my railcar!' Thurston shouted, leading the way while Lacey and Moses tried supporting Judd at the same time. But all the excitement was only a jumble of words and faces swirling around him, because Miller was out on his feet. Only a long sleep, rest and food would make him whole again. The last thing he remembered was being laid down on soft cushions and a feather pillow being pushed under his head, while Lacey pulled covers over him, the tears running down her cheeks.

Judd slept all that day and half the next night, before waking to the soft glow of lanterns inside the warm interior of Thurston's private car. It took a moment for him to remember and realize where he was. Slowly pulling himself up into a sitting position, he saw Lacey on a couch, and the preacher sound asleep in a big chair. At a table next to the couch, F.W. sat poring over Cyrus Toomey's personal papers and records, before he realized Miller had woken up.

'Well, you've had yourself quite a little nap,' he smiled, turning in the chair. 'I trust you're in better shape now than when you rode in?'

Miller rubbed the back of his neck, working out the kinks. 'You have any hot coffee?' He asked.

'I do. Right over there in that silver pot. Would you like me to get it for you, or can you do it yourself? My

148

chef is asleep.'

'No, I'll get it. I need something to wake me up. How about the ledgers, have you looked them all over?'

'I have, and once my lawyers get their hands on them, Mr Cyrus Toomey is going to be measured for a new suit with stripes on it. For how long and in what degree of severity, I can't say. Suffice to say he's going to jail, and maybe far worse than that, on multiple charges, thanks to your unrelenting diligence. If all this works out as I believe it will, it would be well for you to remember it did not take your six-gun to put him behind bars. I realize that in some situations you had no other choice, but nevertheless the law can work for you when it's given the chance.'

'Yea, maybe it can. But for that to happen they'll have to find Toomey first. By now he might not be in Red Bluffs any more. And he has the money to run as far away as he can.'

'Once United States deputy marshals go after him, they'll run him down no matter how long it takes, or how far he goes. Wherever they put their boots down, they are the law and they'll find him sooner or later, you can count on that. And one other thing. Tomorrow morning I'll sign papers to buy your property, and bring my rail line through it. You'll be a man of considerable means after I do so. You might want to begin to think about what you'll be doing next, especially now with Lacey. She's a beautiful young woman, and someone I can also see is a very special person. I'd say you're a lucky man to have her obvious affections, as you do. Together, you two should be able to do anything you want in life. I envy you for it.'

Judd didn't answer. He only smiled and nodded. There was nothing he could add to that.

CHAPTER ELEVEN

Two days later the supply train from back east reached the railhead with much needed new material. F.W. wrote a long and detailed letter to be delivered to his attorney's back in Ohio, along with Toomey's ledgers. His instructions were to set the wheels of justice in motion to find Cyrus Toomey, and bring him to trial on charges of document fraud, embezzlement of public funds, and conspiracy to commit the murder of Randall Miller. He also specifically requested that United States deputy marshals be sent west to track the ex-mayor down, as there was no other law available that far west except in a few widely scattered towns that had their own sheriff, none of whom would ever leave their post to track down anyone. It would take the long arm and money of the federal government to take on this task.

On a quiet Sunday morning before another day of work began, Moses, bible in hand, married Judd and Lacy in Thurston's private car, F.W. marking the event by opening several bottles of champagne from his personal stock. The railroad magnate had invited half a dozen of his foremen to attend, plus the engineers and firemen from both locomotives. At the end of the ceremony, everyone came out on to the flatbed car, to the applause and shouts of the Asian rail gangs, while both engines loudly blew their steam whistles. Later that afternoon Judd informed Thurston that he, Lacey and Moses would be leaving the following day for Red Bluffs. Judd wanted to see his ranch property for the last time, and to make one final ride into town.

'You're welcome to stay here and ride into town in style!' Thurston half kidded, half meant it. 'It will only take a few more weeks before I'm there.'

'We appreciate the offer, but I want to go back and maybe see if Toomey is still around,' Judd countered.

'If he is, you leave that six-gun of yours in its holster. Let the marshals take care of him. You've had enough gunplay to last a lifetime. Besides, you're a married man now, and you have someone else to think about instead of just yourself.'

The following morning Thurston stood on the flatbed ready to blow his whistle to start the work gang. He hesitated a few minutes, watching Moses' wagon with Lacey as passenger and Judd riding alongside, all waving goodbye. The rail king smiled as the trio grew smaller and smaller as they rode away, until they were only dots enveloped by tall prairie grass on the horizon. Then they were gone. He wondered if he'd ever see the cross-draw cowboy again. A small smile parted his lips, as he turned back to his men in their black-buttoned suits and pants, their long, braided hair wound round their box hats, looking up at him, waiting for orders.

'All right, you men. Let's get to it. I want to hear those spike mauls ring like a bell, and see more steel rails shining in the sun out ahead of me!' The locomotive blew three blasts on its loud steam whistle as the rail gangs turned to start a new day's labour.

This time the return journey to Red Bluffs wasn't made at the brutal pace day and night as Judd's previous rides. Moses' wagon served as home when the sun went down, and cooking fires danced to new life. The three of them, bound together by unlikely circumstance, took their time. Two full weeks passed before Moses pulled his wagon to a stop at the burned-out remains of what was once Judd and Randall's cabin, late one afternoon.

Judd eased down out of the saddle. Taking in a deep breath, he surveyed everything around him as old memories came rushing back. The blackened, burned out timbers of what once was the cabin, stood like ghostly fingers pointing to the sky. All this had been his and Randall's dream, to some day make this land into a working ranch. Now those dreams were as dead as the ashes blowing in the sundown wind. Lacey quickly came to his side. Wrapping both arms around him, she studied the look on his face.

'I know what you're thinking,' she whispered. 'You lost everything here, but we can make a new start

153

someplace else, Judd. I swear we will. We've both sur-
vived everything else. We can this, too. I won't let it
stop us, not ever.'

He looked down into her eyes, trying to force a
smile, caressing the back of her neck. 'I thought on
the ride back here that I'd be sort of coming back
home. But now that we're here, it doesn't seem
much like it any more, I'm not sure why. Maybe
because I've sold this place and Randall is no longer
here to enjoy it, too. I want to stay just a few days
while I ride into town, and see if Toomey is still
around.'

'Please, don't do that. Don't tempt yourself into
doing something that could only bring more trouble.
Let the law take care of it, like Farris said it would. It's
not worth taking a chance like that. Not now. Not
after all this.'

Moses came up alongside them while looking
around the property. 'Nice piece of ground, for sure,
Judd. You and your brother made a good pick,
buying it. I'm sure there's more like it around Red
Bluffs where you and Lacey can settle down and have
a passal of kids.'

Lacey blushed, as Judd turned to the tall preacher.
'I might not want to settle anywhere around here,
after all that's happened. I used to think I'd come
back here and start all over again. Now I'm not that
certain any more. It might be better for me and
Lacey to head out someplace else. And what about
you, Moses, what are your plans now?'

'Me? Oh, I'm taking this wagon of mine and

heading back to my place across the desert. I miss it. I guess I never realized how much until I got away from it for so long. I've got my Indians to keep teaching the Good Book to, and any wandering souls I happen to run into. You know how that can happen, don't you?' He raised an eyebrow, in jest.

'Yes, I do.' Judd could not help but smile, before changing the subject. 'I'll have to go into town and buy Lacey a horse and saddle. After we leave here and we part company, she'll need it wherever we end up going. I'll have to get a packer, too.'

'I think that's a fine idea. I'll enjoy your company for at least a few days longer, before we have to say good bye.'

Lacey grabbed Judd's arm squeezing it. 'If you insist on going into town, would you please leave your six-gun here with me? I don't want you to take a chance on using it.' She stared hard into his eyes, pleading with him to say yes, without saying another word.

'It's too late to go in now. I'll ride in tomorrow early. I'm not going to feel comfortable without it, but I'll try, just for you!'

The following morning Judd rode down Main Street in Red Bluffs, to the pointed stares and whispers of men and woman on the street who feared he was back. But he looked straight ahead without so much as a glance at any of them, finally turning off into a narrower back street, where Cyrus Toomey's house stood. The sight of it, as he reined to a stop, brought back an emotional wave of vengeful feelings.

He fought to keep it down, until he saw a paper taped to the front window. Easing out of the saddle, he pushed the wrought-iron gate open and walked up to read the message: 'For sale' it said in big, bold letters. Then under it in smaller writing he read the inked single word, 'Sold'. Cupping his hand against the window, Judd tried peering through the dirty glass pane. The furniture was covered with sheets, and dust covered everything that wasn't. He stepped back. Toomey was gone for sure, out on the run – but where?

At the livery stable Judd bought a pretty bay mare for Lacey, plus a saddle and bridle, and an older, sturdy packhorse. The owner eyed him with fear and suspicion throughout the entire transaction, until Miller handed him the sixty dollars. 'Some folks around here said if you ever came back, there'd be hell to pay, and more killing. Are they right?'

'You see a six-gun on my hip?' Miller countered.

'No, can't say I do.'

'Then I'd say that some "folks" have got it all wrong, haven't they?'

'I reckon they might've.'

'How long has Toomey's house been up for sale?'

'Oh, I'd say for about a month. His daughter Rachel put it up until she finally sold it and left town.'

'Left town for where?'

'She told friends she was going back east to live. I think with relatives. Someone said she stopped at the cemetery before she left on the stage, poor girl. I guess there wasn't much left for her here in Red Bluffs, after what her father did.'

Judd left the livery stable and rode back down the street, leading his pack horse, watched by more people, wondering if he was back to stay. No one dared call out and ask. Not with his reputation. What they could not know was that Judd Miller was done with Red Bluffs, and everyone in it. Everyone he'd fought against was either dead or gone, and now there was nothing left to keep him there. When he passed the last building on the street, he didn't look back. Even some of the hate and vengeance seemed to drift away as the town faded away behind him.

Time would prove that F.W. Thurston was right about the United States deputy marshals. A pair of star men were sent out after Toomey, stopping first in Red Bluffs to see what they could learn by interviewing as many people as possible, and going over his old bank records. From there they rode to Canyon City, after the stage clerk told them about the ticket Toomey had bought, and his question about how much further the stage line went. Four months and two hundred miles later, the determined trackers found Cyrus Toomey living in a run-down hotel in the small town of Humbug.

They made their move early on Sunday morning, even before the sun was up. Obtaining the room key from the hotel clerk, they drew long-barrelled pistols, quietly keyed the lock, and slowly pushed open the door. The soft glow of light from the hall

157

lamp barely lit the darkened room, but it was enough to see Toomey still asleep in bed. The marshals stepped inside and up to the bed.

'Cyrus Toomey, wake up!' one marshal ordered, lowering his pistol in the ex-mayor's face.

Toomey sat straight up in bed, his bleary eyes opening in fear as he tried to understand what was happening to him. He tried to talk, but was still too confused to get a word out.

'We're federal marshals and have a warrant for your arrest, on multiple charges. Get up and get yourself dressed!'

Toomey's trial in federal court in Kansas Territory, two months later, ended in a guilty verdict on all three counts. He was sentenced to twenty years at hard labour, but never served out that time. He died in his prison cell only three short years later. The prison doctor wrote on the death certificate that the cause of death was 'consumption', but Toomey was really a broken man who had seen the good life that he'd schemed and had men kill for, vanish into a cold, dank, six-by-seven foot stone-walled cell. His body wasn't claimed by anyone. He was buried in the paupers' graveyard at the back of the prison, in a field of weeds, stones, and weather-worn wooden markers. The money he was found with on his arrest was claimed by the marshals' service to pay for their long ride tracking him down.

Moses, Judd and Lacey parted company at the edge of the desert that the tall preacher would have to cross. 'You two take care of yourselves. You know

158

I'll miss both of you a whole lot. And Lacey, get a bible and keep this cowboy on the straight and narrow. I won't be around to do it any more.' He smiled, locking hands with Judd, while she squeezed his shoulder. 'If you two ever get the urge to travel, come see an old preacher living in a cave, some time. I've always got room for company.' He waved good bye, flapping the reins down on his mule, as the wagon began rattling away.

The pair watched him go, waving, before turning towards the mountains along the horizon. Judd had said he wanted to go west, and go west they did, riding for over another month until they topped a timbered ridge one day and saw a small, beautiful valley below, bisected by two rushing streams that came together in a foaming, splashing V. Judd knew instantly that it was exactly the kind of ground he'd hoped to find. A log house slowly went up next to tall timber, and the horses were turned loose each evening, to amble away on their hobbles, feeding on the tall meadow grass. In time the spot was named Miller's Crossing by the few other riders who wandered through after them. But with a strong-willed woman like Lacey Miller at his side, Judd was done with wondering what trouble lay beyond the rainbow: he'd finally found a home where a fast, cross-draw six-gun wasn't needed any more to stay alive. Sundown would not come twice on him as it had for all the other men he'd faced in blazing showdowns. All that sundown meant now, was the end of another new day – and a new life, a life he'd once thought he'd never be able to live.

When he walked out of his cabin each morning, the big .45 calibre six-gun was snug in its holster and cartridge belt, hung on a wooden peg next to the door. The days of killing were over. And the time had finally come to put away the anger, too.